D

The bank robber hadn't lost his gun. He pulled it just about the same time as the other horses in the warehouse discovered the open door and ran outside. They raced past Fargo and the robber, knocking him slightly off balance.

Before the man could recover, Fargo had pulled the Arkansas toothpick from its scabbard, flipped it to grab its tip, and thrown it.

The point of the blade hit the robber's chest and kept right on going. It missed the ribs and pierced the man's heart, stopping it instantly. He dropped the pistol and brought both hands to the handle of the knife, as if to pull it from his chest. There was no strength left in him, however, and he fell backward, landing flat on his back.

THE
TRAILSMAN
#355

TEXAS GUNRUNNERS

by

Jon Sharpe

A SIGNET BOOK

SIGNET
Published by New American Library, a division of
Penguin Group (USA) Inc., 375 Hudson Street,
New York, New York 10014, USA
Penguin Group (Canada), 90 Eglinton Avenue East, Suite 700, Toronto,
Ontario M4P 2Y3, Canada (a division of Pearson Penguin Canada Inc.)
Penguin Books Ltd., 80 Strand, London WC2R 0RL, England
Penguin Ireland, 25 St. Stephen's Green, Dublin 2,
Ireland (a division of Penguin Books Ltd.)
Penguin Group (Australia), 250 Camberwell Road, Camberwell, Victoria 3124,
Australia (a division of Pearson Australia Group Pty. Ltd.)
Penguin Books India Pvt. Ltd., 11 Community Centre, Panchsheel Park,
New Delhi - 110 017, India
Penguin Group (NZ), 67 Apollo Drive, Rosedale, North Shore 0632,
New Zealand (a division of Pearson New Zealand Ltd.)
Penguin Books (South Africa) (Pty.) Ltd., 24 Sturdee Avenue,
Rosebank, Johannesburg 2196, South Africa

Penguin Books Ltd., Registered Offices:
80 Strand, London WC2R 0RL, England

First published by Signet, an imprint of New American Library,
a division of Penguin Group (USA) Inc.

First Printing, May 2011
10 9 8 7 6 5 4 3 2 1

The first chapter of this book previously appeared in *Nevada Night Riders*, the three
hundred fifty-fourth volume in this series.

Printed in the United States of America

PUBLISHER'S NOTE
This is a work of fiction. Names, characters, places, and incidents either are the product
of the author's imagination or are used fictitiously, and any resemblance to actual per-
sons, living or dead, business establishments, events, or locales is entirely coincidental.
    The publisher does not have any control over and does not assume any responsibil-
ity for author or third-party Web sites or their content.

The Trailsman

Beginnings . . . they bend the tree and they mark the man. Skye Fargo was born when he was eighteen. Terror was his midwife, vengeance his first cry. Killing spawned Skye Fargo, ruthless, cold-blooded murder. Out of the acrid smoke of gunpowder still hanging in the air, he rose, cried out a promise never forgotten.

The Trailsman they began to call him all across the West: searcher, scout, hunter, the man who could see where others only looked, his skills for hire but not his soul, the man who lived each day to the fullest, yet trailed each tomorrow. Skye Fargo, the Trailsman, the seeker who could take the wildness of a land and the wanting of a woman and make them his own.

*Texas, 1860—where the Trailsman is about to learn
that no matter how bad things seem, they can still go south.*

1

Skye Fargo's lake blue eyes narrowed as the lone rider approached the little train of six wagons the Trailsman was leading from Galveston to San Antonio. Fargo hadn't expected to have a pleasant journey from Galveston to San Antonio, but so far things had worked out much better than he'd thought they would. He didn't want trouble now.

He'd been hired by Louis Charboneau, a New Orleans merchant, to see to it that Charboneau's daughter, Michelle, arrived safely in San Antonio, where Charboneau had opened a new mercantile store. Charboneau had hired a man to watch Michelle on the ship from New Orleans, and Fargo was to take over the job in Galveston.

Thanks to her father's description, Fargo had been prepared for a prim and standoffish young woman who cared nothing for the company of men. He had planned to endure the trip as best he could, since Charboneau was paying well, but he'd received a surprise when Michelle turned out to have quite an interest in him. A personal interest, you could say. Very personal.

Charboneau had been in touch with an immigrant group needing a guide, and he'd gotten Fargo that job, too. Being with the immigrants would give his daughter some extra protection, and Fargo didn't object. It would also give him more money.

Up until now, it was one of the easiest trips Fargo had

ever made. No Indian attacks. No rain to churn up the Texas mud that could slow a wagon down to the pace of a rattler with a broken spine. Not that Fargo would have minded slowing down, since Michelle made his nights very entertaining. So entertaining, in fact, that Fargo almost regretted reaching San Antonio.

But the lone rider bothered Fargo. There was something furtive about the way he held himself and the way he glanced over his shoulder now and then. Fargo decided it would be a good idea to go out ahead to meet him, but first he had a word with Otto Schneider in the lead wagon.

"I don't like that fella's looks," Fargo said. "You be ready for trouble, and warn the others."

Otto was a short, wide man, solid as a butcher's block as he sat on the wagon seat. He was the kind of man Fargo would have liked to have along on any trip he ever made.

"I will do it," Otto said. "Fredrick!" A boy's head popped up behind him. "Jump out of the wagon and go down the line. Tell everyone that there might be trouble."

Fredrick didn't say a word. He slithered to the back of the wagon and dropped off. Fargo nodded to Otto and headed out on his big Ovaro stallion to meet the rider.

The man leaned forward in the saddle as Fargo approached, as if resting himself on his mount's neck.

"I'm hurt," he said, in a voice that was little more than a croak. "Need help bad."

The reins slipped from the man's hand, and Fargo knew he was expected to take them and lead the horse back to the wagons. He wasn't going to do that, however, until he was sure the man was really injured.

They were on a section of the rutted wagon road that was lined with oak trees draped with gray Spanish moss. The trees were so old that their heavy lower limbs touched the ground.

Along with the thick brush that grew among the trees, there was plenty of cover for any friends of the man on the horse.

The man moaned as if begging for Fargo's attention, but Fargo kept his eyes on the trees. He'd heard of similar tricks being played on wagon trains on the way to San Antonio.

Looking off to the right, he detected a slight movement among the thick oaks and saw a brief flash of color that may have been a man's shirt.

Fargo wheeled the Ovaro around and headed back to the wagons.

The man on the horse rose up suddenly with a pistol in his hand. He fired three shots as men on horseback burst from the trees. All of them headed for the wagons, firing their guns as they rode.

The Ovaro threw up clods from its hooves as Fargo passed the first three wagons. The wagons had come to a halt, and Fargo could hear the cocking of rifles.

He pulled back on the Ovaro's reins and stopped the big stallion at the third wagon, where Michelle no longer sat on the wagon seat but lay in the wagon bed. Thanks to Fredrick's warning, she'd been ready to take cover when the shooting started.

The riders had reached the wagons by that time, but the immigrants were ready for them. Rifle fire came from all the vehicles. Fargo pulled his big Henry from its sheath on the Ovaro and jumped into the wagon. He looked back at Michelle, who grinned at him. The girl had spunk. Fargo returned the grin and fired off a couple of shots at the riders, all of whom had concealed their faces with bandannas.

A bullet ripped through the wagon's canvas cover. Michelle said, "Who are those men, Skye?"

"Bandits. They were looking for easy pickings, but they got a little surprise."

Fargo fired the Henry again. His shot hit one of the riders, who fell forward onto his horse's neck, dropping the reins. Another rider did what Fargo hadn't done and grabbed the reins. He turned aside, pulling the wounded man's horse along with him.

The rest of the would-be robbers took this as a signal that they weren't going to get what they'd been looking for, and they all swerved away from the wagons. In seconds they had vanished in the trees.

"Are you all right?" Fargo asked Michelle.

"I am just fine. How could I not be while being guarded by Skye Fargo?"

Fargo laughed and jumped down from the wagon seat. He went to check on the other members of the wagon train. They were all uninjured except for Otto, whose arm had been nicked by a bullet.

"It is nothing," Otto said. "A scratch. Pour a little whiskey on it, a bandage, and it will be fine."

Fargo took a look and agreed. He went back to the Ovaro and sheathed the Henry. He hoped there wouldn't be any more excitement before they got to San Antonio. Except at night. He didn't mind the kind of excitement that Michelle provided, not in the least.

Fargo collected his pay when they reached San Antonio five days later. He and Michelle broke away from the wagon train at the edge of the city and drove right to the brand-new Menger Hotel next to the old Mission San Antonio de Valero, better known as the Alamo.

"I'm sure it's a wonderful hotel," Michelle said, "but I would rather stay with you, Skye, even if it meant sleeping in the wagon."

Fargo didn't recall having gotten much sleep, but he said, "I don't think your father would like that idea."

"Bah," Michelle said, shaking her head. Her black curls bounced under her bonnet. "My father does not like any idea that I might have about men."

Fargo grinned and rubbed his hand over his short beard. "I like your ideas just fine, myself," he said.

"But of course." Michelle gave him a brilliant smile. "How could you not?"

Fargo helped her down from the wagon, and they went into the lobby. Fargo had sent word ahead by a man on horseback they'd met along the way, and Louis Charboneau was waiting there for them, clutching his hat in front of him. He was a corpulent man with a bald head and bulging eyes, and it was clear to Fargo that Michelle must have gotten her trim figure and pretty face from her mother.

Charboneau looked like the prosperous businessman he was—quite a contrast to Fargo, who was dressed in his customary fringed buckskins and wide-brimmed hat, a big Colt in the holster belted at his waist, and an Arkansas toothpick riding in its scabbard low on his leg. Yet somehow Fargo looked just as much at ease and at home as Charboneau did.

Charboneau gave a slight bow in Fargo's direction and allowed his daughter to plant a discreet kiss on the cheek. Michelle would have lingered, but her father sent her back outside.

"I have hired several men to unload your luggage," he said. "You may direct them to be sure there's no breakage. Have them take your things to your room, which is number ten. When our new house is completed, we will live there, but that will not be for another week, or so I am told."

Michelle gave Fargo a lingering look that Charboneau didn't

seem to approve of before she went back outside. Fargo pretended not to notice either her look or Charboneau's reaction.

"Come, Mr. Fargo," Charboneau said after a moment. "We can have a drink, and you can tell me about your journey."

"I'll settle for my pay," Fargo said. "I have to make a call on Marshal Benson before I leave town, and I'd like to see him this afternoon."

"Very well," Charboneau said, and they went to a quiet part of the lobby, where Fargo collected the money owed him.

"My daughter gave you no . . . trouble?" Charboneau said when he handed over the pay.

"Not a bit," Fargo told him. "She was very well behaved."

He didn't smile when he said it, and Charboneau seemed satisfied.

"And there were no bandits? I have heard that the trail can be dangerous."

"There were bandits, but they didn't do any damage to us. We were ready for them."

Charboneau's face darkened. "Michelle was not hurt?"

"Not a bit. She was in the wagon bed and didn't even see anything."

"That's fine, then." Charboneau relaxed and extended a damp, pudgy hand. Fargo shook it. "I wish you well, Mr. Fargo, and I appreciate the good care you took of my Michelle."

"It was my pleasure," Fargo said, and meant it.

He left the hotel and unhitched the Ovaro from the wagon. He mounted up and touched the brim of his hat when he passed Michelle, who gave him another brilliant smile as she told the men to be careful with her valises and trunks.

Fargo rode past the Alamo, where the Texicans had held off Santa Anna for thirteen days back in the war with Mexico. Now the United States Army rented the building from the Catholic Church for a hundred and fifty dollars a month.

Fargo spared a thought for the brave men who had died there twenty-odd years ago, though now it didn't look much like the place where a mighty battle had been fought and lost. Or won, depending on which side you favored.

Fargo made his way through the busy city. The streets were lined with wagons pulled by mules and oxen, and the stench of their droppings filled the air. So did the smoke from blacksmith shops and the smells of leather from saddleries, the freshly sawed wood from the wagonmakers, the hay and grain in the livery stables, the spicy food cooking in the open air.

Stopping at one of the livery stables, Fargo made arrangements for the Ovaro with the proprietor, a man named Fowler, and went back outside. People jostled him as he walked along the busy street. The whole place was much too crowded to suit him. He preferred the plains, mountains, prairies, deserts, and forests to the throngs of humanity in the cities. The noise from the creaking wagons, the braying mules, the hammering blacksmiths, and the talkative multitudes assaulted his ears, and he thought about the silence of a mountain night and the quiet of a desert dawn.

Then he heard the gunshots.

2

Fargo knew the sound all too well. There was no mistaking it for anything else, even in the midst of the other noises of the city.

The shots had come from a street on Fargo's right, and he turned in that direction. He wasn't a man inclined to shy away from trouble.

Several people ran past Fargo, while others took cover behind wagons or in doorways. Fargo had no interest in them. His attention was focused on a building about halfway down the street, the Keller and Smith Bank.

A man ran out of the door. A bandanna hid the lower half of his face, and he held a pistol in his right hand. He looked up and down the street, then fired a couple of shots into the air. The few people who hadn't already gotten out of the way fell down and flattened themselves on the ground.

Except for Fargo, who drew his Colt and kept on walking. The man with the gun didn't see him, or chose to ignore him. He turned and yelled into the bank, and four other men came running out. Each of them carried a cloth sack in one hand and a pistol in the other.

They ran past the man who had called for them, loosened the reins of four horses tied at a hitch rail, and mounted up.

As they were mounting, the lookout man noticed Fargo

for the first time. He fired a shot in Fargo's direction. It chipped the corner of the building on Fargo's right.

Fargo kept walking.

The four men who'd carried bags out of the bank didn't wait around to see what was going to happen. They kicked their horses into motion and fled down the street. Nobody went after them, and just to make sure that they didn't, the remaining man fired a shot over the heads of a couple of men lying in the street nearby.

Fargo was close enough for the man to hear him now, and he called out, "That's four."

"You again," the man said. "You son of a bitch."

He lifted his pistol and took aim, this time steadying the pistol with both hands.

"One shot left," Fargo said, wondering what the man had meant. "Maybe two."

Fargo hoped the man would realize that he was almost out of bullets and that he didn't have much of a chance. If he did realize it, he didn't care. He pulled the trigger.

A bullet tugged at the fringe of Fargo's buckskins. Fargo didn't wait for the man to fire again. He brought up his Colt and pulled the trigger.

Fargo's bullet hit the man in the center of his chest and staggered him. His pistol dropped to the ground. He looked down at the revolver as if surprised to see it there, then collapsed to his knees. From that position, he looked up at Fargo. Fargo met his eyes, but there was nothing in them to see. The man let out a long sigh and toppled forward, landing face-first on the street.

He wasn't going anywhere, so Fargo walked past him and into the bank, reloading his pistol as he entered. A man lay on the floor near the tellers' cages, a pistol not far away from his outstretched hand. A woman lay near him. Two tellers peered over the counter as Fargo came in, and a couple of men crawled from beneath the desks where they'd been hiding.

"Are they gone?" one of the tellers said. He was a thin man with little round glasses.

"They're gone," Fargo said, "except for the one I shot."

The men who'd been under their desks stood up. Both wore black suits.

"Dead?" one of them asked.

Fargo looked at the man on the floor. "Just as dead as this fella."

"He drew his gun," the man said. He tugged at his suit coat to get it back in shape. "Trying to be a hero. He should have known better."

The woman on the floor stirred and sat up. She put a hand to her brow.

"What happened?" she asked.

"You fainted, Miz Martin," the skinny teller said.

"I wasn't shot?"

"No, ma'am. You weren't shot."

"That's good, then." She looked at the man who lay nearby. There was blood on the floor beside him. "Not so good for him, I suppose."

"No, ma'am," the teller said. "Not so good."

Fargo bent and extended a hand to the woman. She took it and stood up with his assistance.

"Thank you," she said, and proceeded to dust herself off.

"Name's Fargo. Skye Fargo."

"Mine's Martin," the woman said. "Frances Martin."

Fargo touched the brim of his hat. "Pleased to make your acquaintance."

Frances Martin smiled, and with what Fargo thought was

frank invitation, which was a little odd considering the circumstances. Or maybe it wasn't odd at all. Escaping violent death at the hands of robbers did funny things to people.

"I'm pleased to make your acquaintance, as well," she said.

Fargo would have taken the conversation further, but a door in the back of the bank opened. A tall man with thinning hair and close-set eyes peered out.

"Well?" he said.

"They're gone, Mr. Smith," the teller said. "Got clean away, except for the one this fella here claims to have shot."

The man looked around the bank. "Is that him on the floor?"

"No, that's Aubrey Franklin," the teller said. "One of our depositors. He went for his gun, and those bastards shot him. Begging your pardon for the language, Miz Martin."

"That's quite all right," Mrs. Martin said. She was paying no attention to the teller, being busy with her appraisal of Fargo.

The bank began to fill up with people wanting to see what was going on, curious now that the danger was past. They chattered in English and Spanish. Fargo paid them no mind.

A voice boomed from the door. "Clear the way. Marshal's coming through."

Fargo turned to see Marshal Harl Benson enter the bank and push through the gathering crowd. The lawman was a burly, middle-aged man with a mostly white mustache.

"What's going on here?" Benson said. He saw Fargo. "Skye Fargo? What the hell are you doing here?"

"Just happened to be passing by," Fargo said.

"You kill that fella outside?"

"Yeah. It seemed like the thing to do, considering that he was trying to shoot me."

"His name was Ken Sevier. Been in a lot of trouble ever since he was a kid, but I didn't think he had the gumption to rob a bank."

"You never know about some people."

"That's the damn truth," Benson said. "Well, tell me what happened, George."

George was Mr. Smith, the man who'd come out of the office. He walked forward now, and began explaining how five men had come into his bank, faces covered and guns drawn, demanding that his tellers fill their sacks with money.

"Naturally I took cover as soon as I could. It was only prudent."

"Yeah," Benson said. "Don't blame you a bit. How much you reckon they got away with?"

"Thousands," George said. He took a handkerchief from a coat pocket and wiped his forehead. "Thousands."

"Well, don't worry about it," Benson said. "We'll get 'em. We got the best tracker in the business right here."

George looked around. "Where?"

Benson stepped over to Fargo and put a hand on his shoulder. "Like I said, he's right here. This is Skye Fargo."

Smith looked blank.

"Damn, George. Didn't you ever hear of the Trailsman?"

Smith shook his head. "Can't say that I have."

"Well, you're a banker," Benson said. "No reason you would have."

"I've heard of him," Mrs. Martin said. "He's supposed to be able to find a trail even where there isn't one. Is that true, Mr. Fargo?"

Fargo looked into her blue eyes. She was younger and prettier than he'd noticed earlier. He told himself that he'd been distracted by the shooting. Otherwise, he'd certainly have noticed the bounce of her blond side curls, the blue of her eyes, the round curves of her body that her dress couldn't quite conceal. He was happy to see that the invitation was still there in those blue eyes.

"There's no accounting for what people say," he told her.

"It's true, all right," Benson said, "but even Fargo can't track men in a city this size. We'd better get started, Fargo, before they get clean away."

"What about the one I shot?"

"I sent a man for the undertaker. Come on."

Benson began shouldering his way through the crowd. Fargo followed along. He'd planned to stop by and see Benson, but he sure hadn't planned on any of the rest of what had happened. He glanced back over his shoulder at Frances Martin, who tilted her head and gave him a smile.

Fargo smiled back. He hoped they'd meet again.

The dead man was gone when Fargo and Benson reached the street.

"Undertaker works fast," Fargo said.

Benson nodded. "He knows his job. That's why the city uses him."

A couple of deputies stood in the street trying to keep the crowd back from the bank.

"All you people get on about your business," Benson said, first in English and then in Spanish. "We got things to do here, and having you around won't help us get 'em done."

It took a minute or so, with Benson glaring at them all the time, but the deputies managed to break up the crowd and send people on their way.

Benson turned to one of the deputies. "Sam, you go inside. Run those people out except for Miz Martin and the men who work in the bank. You talk to them and get the whole story. Find out as much as you can about the men who did the robbery. Descriptions, if you can get 'em. Troyce, you come with me and Fargo. We got to get a posse together."

Fargo had stepped out into the street while Benson was talking. What the marshal had said in the bank wasn't strictly true. It was possible to do some tracking, even in a city, but you needed to get to the tracks before they'd been rubbed out by all the passing feet, hooves, and wheels.

"Why don't you wait to round up a posse?" Fargo said to Benson. "Let's me and you and Troyce see what we can find, first."

"What the hell, Fargo?" Benson was impatient. "We don't have time to be fooling around. We need to get busy."

"That's what we're going to do. You never know when somebody will try to slip one over on you, and this might be the time."

He didn't say anything further. Instead, he started off down the street.

Benson and Deputy Troyce had to hurry to catch up to him. Both of them were a little on the hefty side, and they were breathing heavily when they came up beside him.

"What did you mean about slipping something over?" Benson asked. "And where the hell are we going?"

"I don't know where we're going," Fargo said. "I'm trying to follow the tracks of those bank robbers."

"We don't even have horses," Troyce said. "We can't follow 'em on foot."

"There're too many people," Benson said, looking at the crowded street. "We can't ever find anybody like this."

"Maybe we can," Fargo said. "That's what I meant about slipping one over. If you were those men and you were trying to hide from the law after robbing a bank, why would you even leave town? A town this size has a thousand places to hide, and you don't have to worry about Indians or coyotes or sleeping on the ground. You can even get yourself a good meal if you want one."

"They're bank robbers," Troyce objected. "They're wanted men. The bank'll be putting up a good reward for them. They gotta hide out."

"Why do they have to leave town to do it?" Fargo asked, looking down to make sure he was still following the right tracks. "Nobody knows who they are. Their faces were covered. I don't think anybody in the bank recognized them."

"Well, if they're in town we'll get 'em," Troyce said. "They know that. That Ken Sevier, he had friends. We'll look for them. He had a couple of cousins, too, and both of 'em just as troublesome as he was. I'll bet they were in on it. If they're smart, they'll be halfway to Fort Davis by now."

It was a long, hot, dusty, dry way to Fort Davis, as Fargo was well aware. He didn't think the robbers would want to go that far. Even if they did, they wouldn't have been halfway there or even close to halfway.

"What if it wasn't the cousins or his friends?"

"Well, hell, who else could it be?"

Fargo didn't have the answer for that one, but he said, "Somebody with more gumption than Sevier. His cousins and friends got the sand to rob a bank?"

Troyce had to think about it. "Damned if I know. What d'you think, Harl?"

"Don't know. Hell, one of the cousins is just a kid. The other one's mostly a drunk, like the friends."

"So likely it's somebody else," Fargo said. "You can round up the friends and cousins later and ask 'em if you want to. Right now, we need to keep on looking."

He turned down a side street. Benson and Troyce followed along.

"They don't know for sure I killed Sevier," Fargo said.

"Put out the word he's alive. Maybe they'll come after him to be sure he doesn't talk, try to break him out of jail."

"You know better than that, Fargo," Benson said. "Can't nobody get inside the Bat Cave. Wouldn't even be any use to try."

The Bat Cave was what people called the big two-story building near the Military Plaza. Fargo had been headed for it to see Benson after he'd left Michelle at the Menger. It housed the city marshal's office, as well as the courthouse and jail. Fargo had been inside it a time or two, but he'd never seen any bats. It was dark as a cave, though, back in the cells, and its thick walls and the bars on the cells would keep out the robbers, all right.

"Guess you're right about that," Fargo said.

Benson laughed. "Hell, yes. Anyway, they know Ken wouldn't talk. He's a rascal, but he's not the kind to give up his friends. No use even to try that old trick."

Fargo nodded and turned down another street. He followed the tracks for a ways and went into an alley that ended a block away at a low fence.

"What's down there?" he asked.

"Nothing," Troyce said. "Just another alley that runs behind these buildings."

"That's where the tracks go," Fargo said.

"If you're following the right ones," Troyce said.

Fargo was getting a little tired of Troyce and didn't answer. He didn't need to because Benson said, "He's following the right ones, Troyce. You can take my word for it."

Troyce looked doubtful, but he said, "I guess they could follow that alley down there on out of town if they turned left. Don't know why they'd come this way, though."

"To get out of sight," Benson said, but he didn't sound convinced, either.

On either side of the alley were windowless walls, all of them two stories high.

"What's in these buildings?" Fargo asked.

"They're warehouses," Benson said. "Might be anything. Hay, grain, Lord knows what all."

"We might as well have a look," Fargo said as he started down the alley.

The buildings shaded the alley, and it was cooler here than on the street. The noise was less, too, and Fargo was careful to make no sound as he followed the tracks. When they reached the end of the buildings, the tracks showed that the horses had gone to the left down the wide alley that ran behind the buildings.

"See what I mean?" Troyce said when Fargo pointed it out. "They're headed out of town. Smartest thing they could do."

"Maybe," Fargo said.

He turned left. It was even quieter in back of the buildings, the noise from the street being almost entirely cut off. The backs of the buildings rose up above him. There were large wooden doors where wagons could be easily unloaded. The tracks ended at the first of the doors.

There were other tracks, both those made by horses and those made by wagon wheels, but the only fresh tracks were from the horses Fargo was sure had come from the bank. He pointed them out to Benson and Troyce.

"I'll be damned," Benson said, keeping his voice down. "Looks like you were right, Fargo. They were gonna hide right here under our noses, probably laughin' at the thought of us out there in the desert looking for 'em. How about it, Troyce? Didn't I tell you about Fargo?"

"You did," Troyce said, keeping his voice low as Benson had, "but I didn't put much stock in it. I'm sorry I doubted you, Fargo. You know your business, all right."

"He damn sure does," Benson said. "Let's put an end to this right now."

"There's at least four of them," Troyce said, "and just the three of us. No way we can see what they're up to in there, either."

The building where they stood had windows on this side, but all of them were at about the height of the second story. Fargo thought that maybe there was no second floor, just one big open space inside.

"I'd better go round up some men," Troyce said.

"If you go off," Benson said, "the robbers might take a notion to leave. Then there'd be four of them and two of us. Good as Fargo and I are, that's not good odds. Unless you were planning to take us with you."

Troyce looked sheepish. "I wasn't planning anything. I was just saying."

"I say we take 'em right here." Benson looked at the Trailsman. "What do you think, Fargo?"

Fargo had known Benson for a good while. They'd met before Benson had become the City Marshal, and Fargo knew him to be a good man in a fight but a little headstrong. Once he made up his mind, there was no stopping him.

"You're the marshal," Fargo said.

"Damn right, I am, and I say we're going in."

"Not through this door, though," Fargo said.

"Why the hell not?"

"Bound to be locked," Fargo said. "Look at that window up there." He pointed to a half-open window above them.

"So what?" Troyce said. "We can't get to it."

"I can," Fargo said.

"How?"

"If the marshal will brace himself against the wall, you

can give me a boost up. I can stand on his shoulders and see inside."

Troyce looked dubious, but Benson leaned forward slightly and put his hands against the wall.

"What're you waiting for?" he said.

Troyce looked at Fargo. Fargo shrugged, so Troyce bent down and made a stirrup with his joined hands. Fargo stepped into the stirrup, Troyce heaved, and Fargo stepped onto Benson's shoulders.

Benson was sturdy enough, and Fargo found his eyes just above the level of the windowsill. Dust drifted out of the window and tickled his nose. He could smell horses and hay.

The building was cavernous and the light was dim, but Fargo could see four men at the far end of it. They sat at a table with a bottle in the middle. They all had glasses, and they drank while they talked in low voices. Fargo couldn't hear what they were saying. The bags they'd taken from the bank sat on the floor not far away.

The horses were in the building, too, eating the hay that was scattered all over the floor. Their saddles lay up against the wall.

Fargo saw that a wide balcony extended along all four sides of the building, maybe to help with stacking goods or hay in the warehouse. At the front of the building, a staircase went down from the balcony to the floor.

Fargo dropped down to the alley, and Benson straightened with a sigh of relief.

"You been eating rocks, Fargo?" he said. "You're heavy as a damn mountain."

Fargo grinned and brushed his hand across his bearded cheek. "It's this hair," he said. "Makes me feel heavy."

"Sure," Benson said. "What did you see in there?"

Fargo told him, and Benson said, "How do we go about getting them out of there?"

"I'll go through the window," Fargo said. "You and Troyce come in through the door."

"Door's locked," Troyce said. "You know it is."

"Shoot your way in," Fargo said. "I'll go through the window when you start shooting. They won't think anybody will be above them. We'll outmaneuver them."

He bent down and pulled off his boots and socks so he could climb better, then said to Benson, "You ready?"

Benson sighed and braced himself on the building. "You sure about this, Fargo?"

"I'm sure."

"Let's go, then."

Troyce made a stirrup, and Fargo stepped up on Benson's shoulders. He took hold of the windowsill and pulled himself up so that he could hold himself there with his forearm.

When Benson felt the weight leave him, he stepped away from the wall and pulled his pistol. Troyce followed suit. Benson gave him a nod, and they both fired at the lock.

As soon as they did, Fargo shoved the window up with his free hand. It squealed, but the men in the warehouse didn't hear it. They'd all jumped to their feet, kicked over their chairs, and grabbed for their pistols as soon as they heard the shots. Their attention was focused on the door.

Fargo pulled himself through the window as Benson and Troyce kicked open the door. The four men blasted at the doorway, but Benson and Troyce had jumped aside. The bullets ripped into the wood or flew harmlessly outside.

The horses reared and screamed. Their hooves pounded the dirt floor of the warehouse. They ran in panic around the big open area.

Fargo drew his Colt and ran around the balcony, his bare feet making no noise on the boards. When he reached the right side of the building, he stopped. He had to yell to make himself heard over the noise of the horses.

"It's all over, fellas! Put the guns on the floor and your hands on your heads."

Instead of doing as Fargo ordered, three of the men turned their faces toward him, swung their pistols up, and let loose a barrage of shots. Bullets thunked into the planks, and a couple came right on through.

One of the men, however, dropped his pistol and crawled under the table, maybe hoping it would protect him. Fargo could hear him wailing over the noise of the guns and horses.

Fargo returned fire at the three men. One of them fell back onto the table, and it crashed down on the man beneath it. The man Fargo shot rolled off the table to the floor.

Benson and Troyce charged through the door, blasting away.

The horses ran along the warehouse walls in panic. They nearly trampled the marshal and his deputy, but they jumped back out of the way just in time.

As the horses passed the three men, one of them grabbed the mane of the lead horse and pulled himself up. He rode Indian-style, his body near the wall, his leg hooked over the horse's back. Fargo didn't have a shot at him.

The two men still standing near the table kept shooting at Troyce and Benson, who once again had to jump back as they saw the horseman headed in their direction. They landed on the floor on opposite sides of the door and fired at the two men who still remained by the table.

Fargo holstered his Colt and ran back toward the window. If the rider turned in the wrong direction, he'd get clean away. If he didn't, Fargo had a chance.

The man pulled himself erect in the saddle as he passed through the door and yanked the reins to the left.

Fargo jumped through the window, his hat flying off as he dropped.

He knew at the instant he jumped that he was going to miss the rider. It was too late to change his mind, however, and he didn't miss by much. He stretched out an arm and caught the collar of the man's shirt. He held on as he hit the horse's rump and pulled the man from the animal's back. The horse kept going, but Fargo and the robber hit the ground.

Fargo was on his feet at once. So was the robber, who swung a big fist at Fargo's head. Fargo ducked under it and hit the man with a right to the heart.

The man staggered, and Fargo moved to follow up. The robber stomped Fargo's foot, which wouldn't have been so bad had Fargo not taken off his boots.

Pain shot up from Fargo's foot to his knee, and he bent forward. This time the man's fist didn't miss. Fargo staggered, each step sending new shocks of pain up his leg. His hand went to his holster, but the pistol had fallen out. Fargo didn't see where it had gone.

The bank robber hadn't lost his gun. He pulled it just about the same time as the other horses in the warehouse discovered the open door and ran outside. They raced past Fargo and the robber, knocking him slightly off balance.

Before the man could recover, Fargo had pulled the Arkansas toothpick from its scabbard, flipped it to grab its tip, and thrown it.

The point of the blade hit the robber's chest and kept right on going. It missed the ribs and pierced the man's heart, stopping it instantly. He dropped the pistol and brought both hands to the handle of the knife, as if to pull it from his chest.

There was no strength left in him, however, and he fell backward, landing flat on his back.

Fargo recovered his knife and plunged it into the dirt of the alley to clean off the blood, then wiped it on the man's shirt before returning it to its scabbard.

The warehouse was quiet now, but Fargo didn't plan to go back inside until he'd put on his boots and found the Colt.

He could put on only one boot. His right foot had already begun to swell. If he put the boot on, he'd have to cut it off later. He just hoped his foot wasn't broken, though the way it hurt, it might have been.

Fargo hobbled over to the door, carrying a boot in one hand and his revolver in the other. He looked in from the side of the doorway. Gun smoke hung in the air, its acrid tang overwhelming the scent of hay and horseshit. The man who'd gone under the table still lay there, the table right on top of him. He was still wailing, too. The other two men lay not far away. They weren't wailing.

Benson bent down and grabbed the edge of the table. He heaved it off the man.

"Get up and shut up, you son of a bitch, or I'll shoot you in the back of the head and put a stop to your caterwauling."

Troyce checked the other two men to see if they were alive. They weren't. Fargo holstered his gun and limped in.

"It's just like I thought," Troyce said. "It's Sevier's cousins and his buddies. Never thought they'd turn bank robbers. They won't be robbing any more banks, though."

"Dead?" Fargo said.

"Dead as anybody ever was. What happened to you?"

Fargo told him.

"You kill the son of a bitch?"

"Yeah," Fargo said.

He looked at the other man, the only one left alive. He sat with his hands on his head, looking terrified. He also looked like he was about fifteen.

"What about that one?" Fargo asked.

"One of the cousins," Benson answered. "The one I told you about—the kid. Name's Isaiah, like the prophet. Folks call him Ike."

Ike didn't look much like a prophet. His beardless face was screwed up in grief and tears ran down his cheeks.

"You killed 'em all," he said. He paused to snuffle. "Might as well go ahead and kill me, too. I got nothing left. You've killed ever'body I knew in the world."

"How'd you get yourself into this?" Benson said.

"They told me they'd kill me if I didn't go along," Ike said, his voice cracking. "I knew they'd do it, so I did what they told me."

"Whose idea was it?"

"Ken's. He said it would be easy. He said we'd all be rich and wouldn't have to take any shit from anybody ever again."

Benson rolled his eyes. "And you believed that?"

"I didn't care if it was the truth." Ike's voice cracked. "I just didn't want them to kill me."

"Stand up," Benson said.

"I don't think I can. I might have pissed my pants, too."

Troyce snorted. Fargo couldn't tell if it was a sound of disgust or if Troyce was suppressing a laugh.

"You better get up," Benson said. "Now."

Ike got to his feet. His knees buckled, and he nearly fell, but Benson caught hold of his arm.

"What're you so scared of?" he said.

"I know what they do to fellas like me in the jail. I couldn't stand it. Just kill me. I'd rather die than have that happen to me."

"They don't do that in my jail," Benson said.

"They don't?"

"Hell, no," Troyce said. "Now up at Huntsville, which is likely where you'll wind up, that's a different story. Pretty as you are, you'll be the most popular fella in the place."

The kid put his hands to his face and started wailing again, louder than before.

"Damn it, Troyce," Benson said.

"Just lettin' the kid know what he's in for," Troyce said. "If they don't hang him, that is. Hangin' would be better than Huntsville—that's for sure."

The wailing got louder.

Benson took hold of the kid's shoulder. "Let's go, boy. We'll put you in the Bat Cave for now."

Ike didn't move, so Benson gave him a gentle push to get him started.

"Thanks for your help, Fargo," Benson said as he and the kid passed the Trailsman. "We'd never have got 'em if it hadn't been for you. You better get that foot looked at."

"I'll do that," Fargo said.

"City'll pay the bill."

"Thanks," Fargo said. "One thing bothers me."

"What's that?" Benson asked.

"One of those men seemed like he knew me—the one I had to shoot outside the bank."

"What makes you say that?"

Fargo told him what the man had said.

"You didn't recognize him?"

"No, but the wagon train I was leading ran into some trouble on the way here from Galveston. I wonder if that fella was one of the men who jumped us."

"Wouldn't be surprised. Those Sevier boys are like that. Never believed in working at an honest job if they could cheat or steal and get money that way. That one you killed, he had a bullet wound in the shoulder already, several days old."

"Could've been one of them, all right," Fargo said.

"Probably was," Benson agreed. "We won't have to worry about them anymore, though."

"What about the one who's still alive?"

"You saw what he's like. He won't be any trouble at all."

"I hope not," Fargo said.

3

Fargo knocked on the door of an adobe house shaded by tall cottonwood trees. He hoped he hadn't mistaken the invitation he believed he'd seen in Mrs. Martin's eyes at the bank. His knock was answered by a voice from inside.

"*Quien es?*"

"Skye Fargo."

The door opened only slightly. A woman's round face peeked out.

"We do not know you, señor."

Fargo removed his hat and held it in his right hand. He was holding his boot in the left. "Mrs. Martin knows me."

The woman looked at his boot, then back at his face. "I will ask the señora. The name again?"

Fargo repeated his name, and the door closed. Fargo held his hat and waited. In only a few seconds, the door opened all the way. Frances Martin stood there looking at him.

"Mr. Fargo," she said, "I'm surprised to see you again."

Fargo didn't think she looked surprised at all. "Call me Skye. I hope I'm not bothering you."

Mrs. Martin smiled. "And you can call me Frances. It's no bother at all. Won't you come in?"

She wore the same clothing she'd had on in the bank: a blue dress with a high neckline and long sleeves. The blue matched her eyes.

She stepped aside, and Fargo went into a wide, cool hall-way, making no attempt to disguise his limp.

"My word, Mr. Fargo. Skye. What happened to your foot?"

"I'll be glad to tell you," he said, "but if you don't mind, would it be all right if I sat down first?"

"Certainly it would be all right. Come this way."

Frances led him down the hall and into a big room furnished with a couple of rocking chairs, several leather-covered chairs, lamp tables, and a divan. A shelf against one wall held several books, including a Bible, *Robinson Crusoe*, and several volumes of works by James Fenimore Cooper.

"Please," Frances said, "have a seat."

Fargo thanked her and sat on the divan. He put his boot on the floor near his foot and put his hat on the table beside the divan.

The woman who'd met Fargo at the door came into the room.

"Isabella, please bring us something to drink. Lemonade would be nice."

Fargo would have preferred something a bit stronger, but he didn't complain. The lemonade would be just fine. Isabella brought a tall pitcher that sat on a tray with two glasses. She poured the liquid into one glass and handed it to Fargo. She handed the other to Francis and disappeared with a suspicious glance at Fargo.

The Trailsman sipped his tart drink and explained what had happened after he'd left the bank while Frances sat near him at the other end of the divan.

"My word," she said when he'd finished. "I'm glad you weren't more severely injured."

"It's not really so bad," Fargo said. "I just need a place to rest up for a few days. I was on my way to a hotel when I passed by, so I thought I'd stop and pay my respects."

Fargo hadn't gotten his foot looked at. He'd had worse hurts many a time, and he knew the swelling would go down in a day or so. Even walking on it now didn't hurt him much. He did, however, need a place to stay, so he'd asked Benson where Mrs. Martin lived. Benson told him and volunteered the information that Mrs. Martin lived alone. That was all he'd had to say on the subject, but Fargo could tell there was more to the story. However, he'd heard enough and didn't encourage Benson to continue.

"Why, there's no need for you to stay at a hotel," Frances said. "I have plenty of room here, and it would be inhospitable for me not to offer you a place to stay. After all, you did save my life."

Fargo did his best to look modest and surprised.

"I couldn't ask you to do a thing like that," he said. "Your husband might not like the idea."

Frances's smile disappeared. "I have no husband."

"I'm sorry for your loss," Fargo said.

"Don't be. Gabe was a beast. He deserved what happened to him."

Fargo didn't know what to say to that, so he said nothing. He'd learned that was often the wisest course.

"I know it sounds awful to say so," Frances said, "but he was a terrible man. I never wanted to marry him, but my father insisted." She looked out a window as if staring into the past. "I always obeyed my father."

Once again Fargo kept quiet.

"I killed him, you know," she said.

Fargo's face didn't show anything, but he was surprised to hear it.

"Not my father," Frances said with a small smile. "My husband."

Fargo wasn't doing much to hold up his end of the conversation, but he couldn't think of anything to say. So he just kept quiet. He did wish he'd had a longer conversation about Mrs. Martin with Marshal Benson, but it was too late for that now.

Frances didn't seem to mind Fargo's silence. She said, "My husband was a wealthy man. That was why my father wanted me to marry him. My father needed money. He was hoping for a loan." She looked around the room where they were sitting. "Gabe was my husband's name. Gabe Martin. He bought and paid for all this." She waved her arm to indicate not just the room but the entire house. "He bought it just before we were married, and when we moved in, I thought we'd have a happy life here. That was before I got to know him better."

Fargo decided it was time he said something. "Did your father get the loan he wanted?"

Frances shook her head. The blond side curls shook. "Of course not. Gabe never even considered it, I'm sure. All he wanted was me. Except he didn't really want even me. He just wanted someone to show off at the social events he was obligated to attend thanks to his business. He never considered me a real woman. He even told me that I wasn't woman enough for him."

"Hard to believe," Fargo said.

Frances almost smiled, but she didn't quite bring it off. "Thank you for that, Mr. Fargo."

"Skye," he reminded her.

"Skye. I have a reason for telling you all this, Skye. If you haven't heard of my reputation by now, you'll hear it eventually. I'm the woman who killed her husband and got away with it. The matter never even went to trial."

"I see," Fargo said, but he didn't.

"Oh, it wasn't because they didn't want to hang me," Frances said. "They most certainly did. Everyone liked Gabe. But that was the problem. If they'd tried me, everything would have come out into the open."

"Everything?"

"Yes. Gabe . . . had other women. I wasn't enough woman for him, so he looked elsewhere. Often. Then one night he was . . . entertaining a woman in his bedroom. We had separate rooms, you see, and he often . . . entertained in his own. I was forbidden to go inside."

Fargo was beginning to figure things out. "But you did."

"Yes. One night the woman he was pleasuring became so loud that something came over me. I don't know even now why I did what I did. I knew where Gabe kept his guns, and I got a shotgun. I loaded it and went to the room. Gabe hadn't the decency even to lock the door. I opened it, and they were there, on the bed." Frances paused. "I can still remember the way the moonlight illuminated them as it came through the window."

Fargo thought he knew what was coming, but he waited for Frances to tell it.

"I shot them both," she said. "Only one shot, but it hit the woman too. She was wounded, but not badly. It didn't kill her. Gabe, oh, my. Gabe was a mess."

She paused and looked at Fargo to see if he was shocked. His face showed nothing.

"You can see, can't you, what a scandal it would have been had everyone learned about Gabe?" Frances continued. "I think they all knew the truth, but no one would have spoken of it. Marshal Benson certainly knew after he came here and saw. I sent Isabella for him. He said it was obvious that there'd been a terrible accident. Everyone suspected differ-

31

ently, but they were happy to keep it quiet, even though it meant I wouldn't be punished."

"What about the woman?"

"I paid for her care, and then she went away. I made it well worth her while. And now that you know my story, I'll offer you my hospitality again. I'll understand perfectly if you refuse."

Fargo thought he might have misinterpreted the look in Frances's blue eyes when he'd seen her in the bank . It certainly wasn't there now. He wished he hadn't come to her house in the first place, but now that he was here, he wasn't going to back down. And while she said she wouldn't think less of him if he turned down her offer of a place to say, he didn't believe her.

"I wouldn't think of refusing," he said. "What happened between you and your husband isn't any business of mine, but if you say he got what he deserved, I believe you."

Frances gave him a searching look. "I think you really mean that."

"I'm not in the business of passing judgment. A man who judges other people is too likely to get judged himself."

"Is that from the Bible?"

"Book of Fargo, chapter one."

Frances gave him a faint grin. "I don't believe I've read that book."

"Not many have."

"Maybe I will someday. At any rate, I'm pleased that you'll accept my offer of a room for the night. And dinner, of course. Isabella will be happy to have someone else to cook for. She thinks I don't eat enough." Frances stood up. "I'll show you to your room."

Fargo stood, picked up his boot and hat, and limped after her down a cool hallway to a bedroom with wide windows looking out onto a small garden of flowers and spiky plants. The room held a bed, a chair, and a washstand. A bowl and pitcher sat on top of the washstand.

"This wasn't my husband's room," Frances said. "You needn't worry about that."

"It wouldn't worry me even if it was," Fargo said.

"I didn't think you'd be bothered, but I wanted you to know. Would you like a bath before dinner?"

"Considering where I've been and what I've been doing, it would be a pleasure."

Fargo put his boot on the floor and his hat on the chair. He removed his Colt and the Arkansas toothpick and put them on the chair, too. Frances showed him the room next door where there was a freestanding bathtub, a low table, a chair, a towel rack, and a dressing table. White towels hung on the rack, and there was soap on the low table by the tub.

"I'll have Isabella bring some hot water," Frances said. "You can go ahead and get ready."

Fargo waited until she'd left and closed the door to remove his boots and buckskins. When he was naked, he sat in the tub and waited.

He didn't have to wait long. Isabella didn't knock. The door swung open, and she came bustling in with a bucket of steaming water in each hand. She must have begun heating the water before Fargo had said he'd stay. She'd been sure of him, he thought.

She set the buckets on the floor beside the tub and handed Fargo a piece of soap. She didn't avert her gaze but gave him a frank, if brief, examination and smiled as if satisfied by what she saw.

"The water is hot," she said, picking up one of the buckets.

"That's the way I like it," Fargo said.

He lowered his head, and she poured the water over him.

It was hot, all right, but not scalding, and it felt good as it ran over his body. He could feel himself relaxing, and he knew the hot water would do his foot good, too.

Isabella added the second bucket and left the room without further comment, closing the door behind her. Fargo soaped himself vigorously and was satisfied that he was clean by the time Isabella returned with the rinse water.

Fargo wasn't shy, and he stood up in the tub to take the bucket from her.

"You are much man," Isabella said with clear admiration.

Fargo poured the water over himself and didn't answer. Isabella handed him a towel when he'd finished.

"Señor Martin was a man of your size," she said. "In some ways." She looked below Fargo's waist. "But not all. I will bring you some fresh clothing. I will clean yours."

Fargo didn't protest. He hated to think of what she might bring him to wear, but it would be only for the evening, and no one would see him other than her and Frances.

Isabella picked up his buckskins and left while he dried off with the towel she had given him. When she returned, she handed him a pile of men's clothes and left without a word. Fargo thought she was grinning, though.

He sorted through the clothing and found some drawers, a white shirt, and some pants that weren't too bad. At least they were a solid black instead of plaid like the other pair she'd brought. He put them on and went back to the bedroom. It would have been a bit awkward for him to wear his pistol and knife, so he left them on the chair.

Just as he had everything squared away, Frances appeared at the open door.

"You look . . . different," she said.

Fargo rubbed his beard. "I feel a little funny in these clothes."

"Well, you're much more handsome than Gabe was. Are you ready for dinner?"

Fargo hadn't eaten since morning, and he was ready indeed. Isabella served them fresh tortillas with beans, rice, flank steak, and hot sauce. Fargo ate more than he'd thought possible, and he could tell Isabella was pleased.

After dinner, he and Frances sat in the parlor, and she read to him from *The Deerslayer*.

"I've always been fascinated by the idea of a man making his way in the wilderness. Natty Bumppo must have been a little like you, Mr. Fargo."

"Skye."

"Yes. Skye. A little like you. Have you been alone many times?"

"Often enough."

"Yet you don't appear to be the kind of man who'd ever be lonely, even when you're alone."

She was right, in a way. It was hard to be lonely when you were on the trail because the trees and the mountains were there to keep you company, and the sky and the clouds. But Fargo didn't know how to say that to her. He didn't have the words, any more than Natty Bumppo did.

Frances didn't seem to mind his silence. She closed the book, returned it to the shelf, and said, "I know you must be tired after all you've gone through today. I'll show you to your room."

Fargo could have found the room just fine, but he let her lead the way. At the doorway she said, "Sleep well, Skye."

"I'm sure I will," he said. "Thank you for your hospitality, and tell Isabella I enjoyed the meal."

"I'll do that," Frances said.

Fargo entered the room, and she closed the door gently behind him.

Fargo didn't know how long he'd been asleep when he heard the door open again. Quite a while, he thought. The darkness outside the window was not quite absolute, thanks to the faint glow of moonlight.

He sat up in the bed, and Frances came into the room. Fargo could see well enough to tell that she wore only a thin white cotton gown.

"You're awake," she said.

"I heard you come in."

She walked over to the bed. Fargo saw her clearly now. The gown clung to her curves, outlining her jutting breasts and the swell of her hips. Her rigid nipples pushed against the thin fabric. Her blond hair fell around her shoulders.

Fargo wore no nightclothes. He felt a familiar stirring underneath the sheet that covered him as his shaft began to stiffen.

"My husband told me that I wasn't enough woman for him," Frances said.

"I remember," Fargo said, his throat a bit dry.

"I've often wondered if that was my fault or his own."

Fargo sat up a little straighter in the bed, thinking he might reduce the size of the tent that the sheet was forming as his shaft rose.

"I'm sure it was his fault," Fargo said.

"It's been a year since I . . . since he died. I've hardly noticed men in that time. Until today. When I saw you in the bank, I wondered about you. The Trailsman. I've heard of you."

"So you said."

"I thought you might be the kind of man who could tell me if my husband was wrong, but then you were gone. I thought I'd never see you again."

The sheet was fully tented now, but Frances didn't seem to notice. Fargo, of course, didn't mention it.

"Then you came to my door," Frances said. "I had to tell you the truth about myself, but you stayed anyway."

"I'm a brave man," Fargo said.

"I'm sure you are. But what else are you?"

Frances didn't wait for an answer. She bent down, gripped the hem of the gown, and pulled it over her head. It dangled from one hand for a second before she let it fall to the floor.

Fargo admired her beauty. The blond hair on her head was matched by the golden curls covering her mound. Her breasts were firm and high.

She bent again, this time to pull back Fargo's sheet.

"One thing I am is ready," Fargo said.

"I can see that. Readier than Gabe ever was. I'm ready, too."

With that, she leaned over and took Fargo's steely pole into her mouth. She closed on him, her lips a fiery ring. For a couple of seconds she held him like that. Then she started to move, slowly at first and then faster. Fargo felt himself stiffen even more, though only seconds before he would have said that wasn't possible. Frances hummed in her throat, a satisfied "Ummmmmm" that almost caused Fargo to explode.

Just as things were about to move beyond his control, Frances released him and stood above him, smiling.

"You liked that," she said.

"I did."

"Good. Don't move."

Fargo didn't move, and Frances climbed onto the bed. She straddled him and took his stone-hard staff in one hand.

"Isabella said you were much of a man."

"I didn't think she'd go spreading the word."

"I asked her."

Frances raised herself above him. She paused for a second, letting him anticipate a bit before she lowered herself onto him. There was no hesitation then. She took him inside all the way, joining the wiry hairs of their sexes.

She let Fargo enjoy the sensation of warmth enveloping him and then leaned forward, allowing her hot nipples to brush his stomach before moving them within reach of his lips.

He touched each one with his tongue before taking one engorged nipple into his mouth. Frances gasped as he stroked it with his tongue. He released it and cupped both breasts with his hands, capturing the nipples between thumbs and forefingers.

"Ah," Frances said. "Ah, Skye."

She moved on him, just a little. It was enough to cause a small spasm at the base of his spine, so she did more. She lifted herself slowly until only the tip of his shaft remained inside her.

"Ah," she said again, and lowered herself.

Fargo released her breasts and kept still as she lowered and raised herself with increasing speed. She moved her head from side to side, her hair whipping her face. Fargo thrust into her, matching her speed and desire. He knew she was close to the moment she sought, but he wasn't sure he could hold back his own climax for much longer.

Frances stopped moving. She threw back her head, her mouth wide, though no sound came out. Fargo knew the time had come, and he thrust once, twice, three times.

"Ohhhhhhhh!" Frances said, and Fargo let go, pouring himself into her again and again.

When it was over, she collapsed on him, pillowed by her breasts, but Fargo didn't withdraw. He was already stiffening again as he rolled her over, and with him on top he began to move slowly on her. She responded at once, moving her hips in time with his own motion. In seconds they were rocking together, their speed increasing, and Frances cried out, "Now, Skye, please, now!"

Fargo felt his essence surge out of him again, and Frances thrashed beneath him, her own climax shaking her from the top of her head to the soles of her feet.

When it was over this time, they lay side by side, not speaking. They stayed like that for a while, and Fargo's breathing slowly returned to normal. After a while, Frances said, "I don't think I've ever felt anything like that before."

"It was something, all right," Fargo said.

"Gabe never made me feel that way. Maybe he couldn't. Maybe that's why he needed the other women. They made him feel like more of a man because he paid them to."

"Could be," Fargo said. He'd heard of men like that. Unless they were paying for it, they didn't think they were getting value. "He sure missed out, though."

"You really mean that?"

"I wouldn't say it if I didn't. You're a lot of woman, Frances."

"Then thank you for the compliment."

"Thank you for everything else."

Frances laughed. "Do you think your ankle will be healed enough for you to leave tomorrow?"

Fargo pretended to think it over. "I don't expect it will. It might take quite a while for it to be right again."

"That's good. I'll do my best to make sure you enjoy yourself."

"I do appreciate that," Fargo said. "How do you plan to do it?"

"Let me show you a few ways," Frances said. "If you're up to it." She looked below his waist. "And I do believe you are."

"Looks that way," Fargo said. "You'd better start showing me."

She did.

Ike Sevier didn't enjoy himself that night. He got a cell of his own, but he lay on the bunk and whined and cried most of the night, proclaiming his innocence even when there was no one around to listen to him. The next morning, Troyce spoke to Benson about it.

"I swear, Marshal," Troyce said, "all that caterwauling and moaning is gettin' on my nerves, and it's bothering everybody else in here, too."

"Most everybody else is a prisoner," Benson said. "Just tell 'em it's part of the punishment."

"I'm not a prisoner," Troyce said. "I ought not to have to listen to it."

"You'll be out on patrol in a few minutes, and it won't matter," Benson told him.

"What about me?" Alvie Vernon said, walking up with his mop and water bucket. "I got to clean the floors in this place while I listen to that baby cryin' in there. I can't hardly do the job right if I have to listen to that kind of carryin' on."

Alvie was a small bowlegged gent whose scraggly white beard hid most of his face. He was a deputy, but he was past the age when Benson relied on him to do anything dangerous. He cleaned up around the jail and occasionally locked up a drunk, but that was the extent of his responsibilities.

"Maybe Ike could give you some help," Benson said. "If he's pushing a mop around, he won't have time to think about how bad off he is."

Troyce listened to the whimpering from the cellblock for a second or two longer. "I don't care what you do with him, but if I was in charge, I'd just stuff a sugar tit in his mouth.

40

Either that or shoot him outright. Not up to me, though. I'm leaving to walk my patrol."

When Troyce was gone, Alvie set his bucket down and dipped the mop in. "I don't need no help. I can handle this job just fine."

"I know you can," Benson said. He went and sat at his desk. "But a man can always use some help."

"I know what you think. You think I can't handle my job anymore, and I don't mean the moppin'."

"I never said that."

"Didn't have to say it." Alvie leaned his weight on the mop handle. "You was thinkin' it, though. Mop, sweep, clean up after the prisoners, that's all I'm good for now. Might's well admit it."

"Damn it, it's bad enough I got to listen to Ike Sevier, and now you're starting in on me."

Alvie went right on talking as if Benson hadn't spoken. "Troyce, now, he gets to go out on patrol. Walk around, let people see his badge, get some respect from the folks in town. Not me. Me, I'm stuck in this place. Get no respect from anybody a'tall."

"I respect you," Benson said.

"Not very damn much." Alvie held up the mop. "Otherwise you wouldn't have me wranglin' this damn mop ever' day."

Benson sighed. "All right, I'll tell you what. I'll put Ike on that mop and let you go out with Troyce. He could use some help. How's that?"

Alvie wasn't going to let him off the hook that easily.

"Troyce's gone already. Anyhow, that kid don't look to me like he can find his butt with both hands, much less handle a mop."

"Anybody can handle a mop, and you can catch up with Troyce easy enough. You know the route he walks."

41

"Well," Alvie said, appearing to give it some thought. "You really think Troyce needs my help?"

"Damn right, he does. You go on. I'll talk to Ike."

"Well, I guess I'll do it if you say so."

"I do. Get out of here."

"Wouldn't want to leave you shorthanded here if you don't really mean it."

"I mean it," Benson said. "I'm not going to tell you again. Get out of here and give Troyce a hand."

Alvie grinned and left. Benson got the keys and went into the cellblock. He stopped in front of Ike's cell. Ike was on the bunk, lying on his side, his face turned to the wall. He was no longer making any noise, but his shoulders shook as if he were weeping silently.

"Look here, Ike," Benson said. "There ain't no use for that kind of carryin' on. You got a cell all to yourself, and no-body's laid a hand on you."

Ike turned over and looked at him with tear-filled eyes. "I'm going to prison, Marshal, for something that was no fault of mine." His voice broke. "I let my cousins talk me into that robbery because I thought they'd kill me if I didn't go along. I wish they'd just shot me to start with and been done with it. I'd be better off."

"Still harping on the same string, eh?" Benson said.

"What else can I say?"

Benson shrugged, and Ike turned his face to the wall again.

"Well, hell," Benson said, "you tell your story to the judge. Maybe he'll let you off. Meantime, you can help out around the jail a little, and I'll put in a good word for you."

Ike didn't move but he said, "You'd do that?"

"Yeah, I would. You're young, and everybody knows about those cousins of yours. They were bad to the bone, but you still got a chance to make something of yourself. If the judge feels that way, too, you might get off without going up to Huntsville."

Ike turned back to face Benson and swung his legs off the bunk. "Mopping's all I have to do, and you'll speak up for me to the judge?"

"That's right."

Wiping his eyes and face on his shirt sleeves, Ike stood up. "I'll do it, then."

"Good," Benson said, fitting the key into the lock on the cell door. "It'll be good for you."

"You're right," Ike said. "It'll be real good."

As he stepped through the cell doorway, he put his hand on the nearest bar, gripped it, and slammed the door back into Benson's face as hard as he could.

One of the bars caught Benson's nose, smashing it. Blood poured out and got on Ike's hand, but he didn't mind. He pulled the door back, and as Benson staggered, Ike hit him with it again, this time breaking several teeth and putting a sizable dent in Benson's forehead.

Benson collapsed to the floor, choking on blood. Ike looked at him for a second or two before walking over and plucking the marshal's pistol from its holster.

"You shouldn't have let me out," Ike told him. "You don't have anybody to blame but yourself."

Benson coughed out something that might have been words, but Ike wasn't listening. He thumbed back the hammer of the pistol, pointed the barrel at Benson's head, and pulled the trigger.

The echo of the shot rattled around the jail, and gun smoke hung in the air. The prisoners in the other cells yelled and beat on the bars with their tin cups. Some of them begged Ike to take the keys and let them out.

Ike ignored them. If they weren't smart enough to get out

themselves, to hell with them. He stuck the pistol in his belt and walked out of the jail into the busy street. No one there appeared to have heard the shot through the thick walls of the jail, and Ike saw no reason to stick around. He walked calmly away as if he was just out for an early-morning stroll. After he'd gone half a block, he started to whistle "The Yellow Rose of Texas." It looked like it was going to be a nice day.

4

Antonio Sanchez hardly noticed the smooth-faced young man who whistled as he passed him. Antonio was on his way to speak to Marshal Benson about his neighbor, who, Antonio believed, had either killed or stolen Antonio's dog. Antonio wasn't sure which, but he was sure the dog was missing, and he wanted to see justice done. Marshal Benson was the man to see about justice.

Except that Marshal Benson lay dead on the jailhouse floor in a pool of blood. Antonio stood there and looked at him for a full minute, not knowing whether to stay or run. It never entered his mind to report the murder. Justice for his dog was one thing. Justice for the death of a marshal was likely to be something else entirely, something that Sanchez wanted no part of. He certainly had no desire to join the prisoners in their cells, and he wouldn't have been surprised if they'd all joined together to accuse him of the crime.

By now he'd forgotten about his dog. He turned and fled from the building, the yelling of the prisoners following him as he ran.

Alvie hadn't been able to catch up with Troyce, so he'd given up and headed back to the jail. He'd been thinking about Ike doing the mopping and how he might need a supervisor. Alvie was good at supervising.

He hadn't counted on bumping into anybody, but Antonio Sanchez was headed somewhere in one hell of a hurry. He collided with Alvie and nearly knocked him down.

"I beg your pardon, señor," Sanchez said, and started to hurry away.

He didn't get anywhere, because Alvie grabbed both his arms to steady himself. Alvie recognized Sanchez, who came into the jail every now and then to complain about the trespasses of his various neighbors.

"Where the hell are you goin' in such a rush, Sanchez?" Alvie said.

"Oh, it is you, Deputy," Sanchez said. "I did not see you. I was in a hurry because I was looking for you."

"Me?" Alvie said. "Nobody ever looks for me."

"It is the marshal," Sanchez said. It was too late to conceal the murder now, so he thought it best to appear to have been looking for someone to tell all along. "Someone has killed him."

Alvie shook his head. "You oughtn't make a joke like that, Sanchez. It's not funny."

"I am not making a joke," Sanchez said. "I only wish that I were. You can see for yourself that what I say is true. Just go to the jail."

"You'd better come with me," Alvie said. "Show me what you're talkin' about."

"You will see for yourself. I must go now."

"You must go with me." Alvie still had hold of one of Antonio's arms. "Come on, Sanchez. Let's see what's really going on."

"It is as I told you."

Alvie couldn't believe it. Who'd go into the jail and kill the marshal? Couldn't be anybody in all of San Antonio with the ncrvc to do such a thing, and nobody already in the jail could've done it.

Alvie started down the street, half pulling and half dragging the reluctant Sanchez. When they reached the jail, Sanchez flatly refused to go inside.

"You'd better be standin' right here by this door when I come lookin' for you, then," Alvie told him. "I know where you live, and I'll come after you if you take off."

Sanchez nodded and looked so miserable that Alvie almost felt sorry for him. Alvie went on inside, and when he saw the marshal he had to sit down in the chair at Benson's desk while he tried to take it all in. The prisoners weren't yelling now. The jail was quiet as a tomb, which it was, in a way.

Alvie stood up and went back to see if Sanchez was still at the door. He was there, all right, holding his hat in his hands, twisting it around and around.

"You know Troyce?" Alvie said.

"The big deputy," Sanchez said. "I know him."

"You go find him. You get him here. Ten minutes. No more."

"I do not know where to look."

"I don't give a damn about that. You find him. You hear me?"

"I hear you," Sanchez said.

"Then get goin'."

Sanchez got going. Alvie watched him for a couple of seconds, then went back inside, which is where Troyce found him, sitting in Benson's chair. It had been fifteen minutes since Sanchez had gone to look for him, but Alvie didn't know how much time had passed.

"Jumping Jesus," Troyce said, "what kind of crackbrained brute would do something like that? What the hell happened, Alvie?"

"Ike killed him," Alvie said.

"Ike? That crybaby? Don't give me that, Alvie."

"It was Ike," Alvie said. "His cell's empty. The marshal went to let him out to do the mopping, and Ike killed him."

"Bullshit."

"I know it sounds like bullshit, but that's the way it happened. I asked Blue Johnson. He's in the cell next to where Ike was."

"Blue Johnson wouldn't tell the truth if his life depended on it."

"The hell he wouldn't," Alvie said. "And his life did depend on it." He patted the holster at his side and the old Navy Colt it held. "I'd have shot him if he hadn't told me, and he knew it."

"Where in hell were you when all this was going on?"

"Lookin' for you. The marshal told me you might need some help, and he was gonna let Ike do the moppin'. Thought it might take his mind off his troubles."

Alvie didn't mention that he'd encouraged Benson. He felt pretty bad about that.

Troyce edged his butt onto the desk. "I can't believe this."

"You better believe it," Alvie said. "You're in charge of things now that the marshal's dead. Where's Sanchez?"

"He wouldn't come in. I told him to wait outside. Why?"

"I'm gonna send him for the undertaker. What do we do after that, Troyce?"

"Damned if I know," Troyce said.

Alvie left the deputy sitting on the desk and went outside where Sanchez was still standing but not looking happy about it.

"You don't have to worry none," Alvie told him. "I know you didn't have anything to do with it."

Sanchez pulled a handkerchief from his back pocket and wiped his sweating face. "Thank you, señor."

"You can do me a favor, though," Alvie said. "Go down to Burcell's place and tell him we got a customer for him. You don't have to tell him who it is, though."

"I will do it," Sanchez said. "You know who killed the marshal?"

"Some damn baby-faced kid," Alvie said, and went back inside to where Troyce still sat.

"We can't let that damned Ike get away with this," Alvie said.

"I know it," Troyce said, "but how're we gonna catch him?"

"What about that fella who helped you catch him the first time?"

"Fargo?"

"Yeah, that's the one. He's supposed to be a tracker, and he and Benson were friends. Might be he'd like to help us out."

"If he was to do any tracking, he'd need a trail. I don't expect Ike left one. I don't even know where to start looking."

"You got a better idea?"

Troyce admitted that he didn't.

"You reckon Fargo's still in town?"

"He asked the marshal about Frances Martin, like he might go courtin' her. Maybe he did. You could ask her if she knows where he is."

Alvie glanced at the marshal's body. "Gonna be a real hoo-raw when word about this gets around."

"You don't want to be here, do you?"

"Nope. I'll go see what Miz Martin knows. You better start thinkin' about how you're gonna run the law around here."

Troyce didn't respond, and Alvie left. He passed Hap Burcell, the undertaker, who was on his way inside.

"What happened?" Burcell asked. "You lose a prisoner?"

"Little bit worse than that," Alvie said.

"How much worse?"

"You'll see," Alvie told him.

* * *

Fargo sat on the divan with his foot propped up on a low stool. There was hardly any swelling in his ankle now, maybe none at all, but Frances had insisted that he pamper it.

"You must want it to heal up so I can get out of here," Fargo said.

"Maybe you don't need the stool, after all," Frances said. "And maybe I need to give your ankle a little kick."

Fargo grinned. Isabella had prepared a big breakfast of *chilaquiles* with beans and tortillas. Fargo had eaten more than he'd thought possible, and his mouth was still slightly on fire from the spicy food in spite of all the water he'd drunk with his meal. He wondered what she'd serve for lunch.

"Don't worry," he said. "I don't plan to leave for a while. I haven't hired onto any jobs, so I can do what I please."

"Can you do what *I* please?"

"That would be my pleasure," Fargo said, just as there came a loud knocking at the front door.

Isabella bustled through the room to answer the knock, and she was back in seconds. "A man wishes to know about Señor Fargo. What shall I say?"

"Who is the man?" Frances asked.

"He is one of the marshal's deputies. I do not know his name."

"Ask him to come in, then," Frances said, and Isabella did.

Alvie stood in the room, his battered hat in his hands, and introduced himself. Frances welcomed him, and he thanked her. Then he looked at Fargo.

"Looks like you're laid up," Alvie said. "Might not be much use to me."

"Use for what?" Fargo asked, curious.

"Well, it's like this." Alvie looked at Frances. "You might not want to hear this, Miz Martin."

"Nonsense. I saw a man shot dead beside me yesterday,

Mr. Vernon. I'm sure nothing you have to say can shock me."

"Yes'm, you're prob'ly right about that. So here's the way it is, Mr. Fargo."

"No need for the *Mister*," Fargo said. "Just tell it."

"You remember that Ike Sevier you helped the marshal catch for that bank robbery, I guess."

"I remember."

"Well, he killed the marshal. Shot him in the head and broke out of jail."

Fargo sat up straight, moving his foot from the stool to the floor. If it twinged, he didn't notice it. "Harl's dead?"

"Sure enough, and that Ike's the one done it. The marshal let him out to help mop up the jail, and Ike got his gun."

Harl had been going soft on the kid right from the start, Fargo thought. Harl was a good man, but he should've known better.

"Seein' as how the marshal was your friend," Alvie said, "Troyce and I thought maybe you'd help us track him down."

Frances looked at Fargo and nodded.

"I'll do it," Fargo said. "How soon do we start?"

"Soon as we can. I'll go back to the jail and tell Troyce. You can meet me there."

After he'd gone, Fargo got ready to leave. It didn't take long.

"You'll come back, won't you?" Frances said.

"You can count on it."

"I think there might be a few things that we left undone."

Being a gentleman, Fargo had nothing to say about that.

"Thank you for coming to see me, Fargo," Frances said. "You made me feel like a woman again."

"I felt plenty, myself."

"I'm glad. You take care of yourself. Don't let Ike Sevier get you like he got the marshal."

"Not a chance," Fargo said.

* * *

When he arrived at the jail, Benson's body was gone. The only things left of him were a dark stain on the floor and a little bit of a bad smell in the air. Troyce and Alvie were talking to a man who twisted his hat in his hands as he spoke to the deputies.

"I tell you, it was the very man. The one with the smooth face of a child. He whistled as he walked, and it could be no other."

Troyce looked over and saw Fargo. "Glad you could help us out, Fargo. This fella here is Antonio Sanchez. He says he just saw the man who killed the marshal."

"It was not fifteen minutes ago, señor, in Rosita's place. He was talking to some other men. Not men who looked like him."

"What did they look like?" Fargo asked.

"Hard. They were hard men."

"What were you doing there, anyway, Sanchez?" Alvie asked.

"After what I saw in here," Sanchez said, gesturing toward the stain on the floor, "I needed a drink."

"Why in that place?"

"It is not so far from my home."

"I'd look for somewhere else to drink if I was you," Alvie said.

"If it's close to your place," Troyce said, "why would Ike Sevier be there?"

"He seemed to know those men. That is all I know. I thought I should tell you."

"What do you think, Troyce?" Alvie said. "Worth havin' us take a look?"

"How much tequila did you have?" Troyce asked Sanchez.

52

"None, not a single drop. When I saw that man, I left and came straight here."

"I guess it's worth a look, then," Troyce said. "You and Fargo can go, Alvie. Sanchez can show you the way."

"I know where Rosita's is," Alvie said, and Sanchez looked relieved. "You don't mind goin' with me, Fargo?"

Fargo didn't mind, and the two of them left, followed by Sanchez.

"Rosita's place isn't in the best part of town," Alvie said as they made their way along the crowded street. "It's mostly the kind of place you want to stay out of."

"What's Ike Sevier doing there, then?"

"Well, that's a mighty good question. Maybe we'll find out the answer."

They soon left the crowds behind, and the streets became more winding and narrow as Alvie led Fargo down by the river and into the part of town that most gringos chose to avoid. Sanchez turned down a side street and disappeared without a farewell. Eventually they came to an adobe building with a low, flat roof and the word *ROSITA'S* painted in ragged red letters on the wall above the doorway. There was no actual door that Fargo could see, just an opening. He and Alvie went right inside.

The place was noisy and crowded even though it was still the middle of the morning. Things started to quiet down, however, as soon as Fargo and Alvie stepped through the door. Fargo looked around.

There was no real bar, just some boards laid atop four barrels. A rickety shelf behind the makeshift bar held only a few bottles, and they all looked the same—tequila for sure, Fargo thought. The bartender was almost as short and round as the barrels, but he wasn't fat. Just solid.

The room smelled of liquor, sweat, and the cheap cheroots

most of the men were smoking. What light there was came in through the doorway and a couple of small windows.

Fargo didn't see Ike Sevier. It was completely quiet now, and everybody looked back at Fargo. Their faces were hard, as Sanchez had said, and they all had hard eyes, too—the kind that had seen a lot, most of it bad. Not that the men would have minded. Men with eyes like that would have done plenty of bad things themselves without a second thought.

Fargo wasn't intimidated, though, and neither was Alvie. He walked over to the bar. The bartender turned away and pretended not to see him.

"Hey, Rosita," Alvie said when he reached the bar. "How about a drink?"

The bartender turned slowly back to face him. "My name is not Rosita."

"That's the name over the door. Thought maybe you was Rosita."

"You are not funny."

"Maybe not, but I'm a deputy marshal, so you might want to be a little more polite to me."

The bartender looked over Alvie's head at the men seated at the tables. "This man is a deputy marshal. We should all be afraid of him."

Nobody said anything, but a few of the men smiled. They weren't cheerful smiles.

Alvie wasn't bothered. He pointed over his shoulder with his thumb. "That's my friend Fargo back there. We're here looking for Ike Sevier."

"I never heard of that man."

"He was in here a few minutes ago. You'd remember him. Don't look like he's even old enough to shave."

The bartender shrugged. "I have not seen him."

Fargo continued to look around the room. One corner was

especially dim, and it appeared to Fargo that someone was hunkered down behind the men at the table. The men there avoided Fargo's eyes, but they looked ready for trouble. They even looked like trouble would make them happy. A man near Fargo spit on the floor. Considering the condition of the floor, he wasn't the first to do so.

"How about it, Fargo?" Alvie called from the bar. "You reckon Ike's in here?"

"Could be," Fargo said. "Let me take a look."

He started toward the table in the corner. The man who had spit on the floor waited until he was about to pass his table and quickly stuck out his foot.

Fargo might have fallen if he hadn't been ready for something like that, but he'd been in rooms full of trouble before and knew what kind of tricks to expect. He kicked the man's boot aside. The man jumped up, and Fargo pushed him back down into his chair without a word.

The other men at the table jumped to their feet, but before they could attack Fargo a pistol shot and the sound of a bottle breaking shattered the silence.

"I don't want to hurt any of you folks," Alvie said, "so I won't shoot you. But if anybody else makes a move, I'll break ever' damn bottle of tequila on Rosita's shelves."

"My name is not Rosita," the bartender said.

Fargo grinned as the men sat back down. He pulled out his own Colt and went past that table and the next without further incident. When he reached the table in the corner, Ike Sevier rose up from his hiding spot. He looked as innocent as a schoolboy who was about to put an apple on the teacher's desk. He didn't have an apple, however. Like Alvie and Fargo, he held a gun in his hand.

"I'm getting damn tired of you turning up everywhere I go, Fargo," Ike said.

Fargo nodded. "Don't blame you. I'm getting tired of having to come after you."

"I'll just kill you, then," Ike said. "Save us both a lot of trouble." ·

"You can try," Fargo said, "but it's two guns against one. Either Alvie or me's going to get you, too."

"Damn," Ike said. "You could be right about that. So I'll just kill this fella."

Snake quick, he dropped the barrel of his pistol and pulled the trigger. The shot crashed, and the head of the man seated in front of Ike flew apart. Blood and bone spattered everyone at the table, and the room erupted all around Fargo with men leaping out of chairs, yelling, kicking over tables, drawing pistols and knives.

Fargo would have triggered a shot at Ike, but the baby-faced man was already lost in the seething mob. Fargo ducked to avoid a chair being swung at his head and slammed his gun barrel into the knife hand of a man who was trying to gut him.

A man leaped on Fargo's back and got a weak choke hold on him. Fargo holstered his gun, then reached back and grabbed the man's shirt with both hands. As the man tried to increase the pressure on Fargo's windpipe, the Trailsman did a quick lean and flipped the man forward, breaking his hold and flattening him against the wall.

Fargo heard more shots as he turned to look for Ike in the mob. He caught a glimpse of him leaving through the door, but when he started in that direction, two men loomed in front of him, both of them holding pigstickers that made Fargo's Arkansas toothpick look small.

Fargo put up both hands in a gesture of peace. The men grinned, showing tobacco- and tequila-stained teeth with gaps between.

Fargo kicked the one on his left in the knee, which tried to bend backward. That being impossible, the kneecap cracked like a tree branch, and the man fell into the hombre next to him. Fargo took advantage of that by slapping the second man's knife aside and punching him in the center of his chest.

The man Fargo had kicked lay in the floor clutching his knee as the second man fell on him, gasping for a breath that wouldn't quite come.

Fargo pulled his pistol in case anybody else got any ideas about stopping him. Nobody seemed to want to, and the fighting ceased. A couple of men dragged the fallen knife wielders out of Fargo's way, and Fargo looked over at the bar.

Alvie stood at the bar, pointing his gun at the bartender who held an ax handle in his hands. Alvie looked wobbly. His hat lay on the floor.

"Put that ax handle down, Rosita," Fargo said.

The bartender laid the handle on the bar. "My name is not Rosita."

Fargo ignored him. "You okay, Alvie?"

Alvie holstered his gun, picked up his battered hat, and rubbed his head.

"I guess so." He looked at the hat, then at the bartender. "Woulda brained me if it hadn't been for my hat." He settled it on his head. "Used to be a damn good hat, but just look at it now. All busted up. You owe me a new one, Rosita, you son of a bitch."

The bartender didn't bother to correct Alvie about his name. He just sighed.

"You can pay me later," Alvie said. "Let's get out of here, Fargo."

Alvie walked to the door a bit unsteadily, but he did better as he went along. Fargo looked back at the room one last time. The only sound was a quiet moan from the man with the broken kneecap. Nobody seemed too concerned about the man Ike had killed, least of all Alvie.

"Wait for me outside," Fargo said. "I need to talk to some of these fellas."

"You sure you don't need my help?"

"Not as much as you need some fresh air."

Alvie pulled out his old Colt and stood in the doorway. "I can breathe pretty good right here. Anybody tries anything, I ain't messin' around. I'll just kill 'em." He looked at the bartender. "That means you, Rosita."

"My name—"

"You shut up," Alvie said, and the bartender did.

Fargo went back to the table where the dead man lay on the floor. Parts of his head still marred the table, but nobody paid the mess any attention.

Fargo looked at the men who sat there and said, "What did Ike Sevier want?"

Nobody answered.

Fargo stuck the end of his pistol barrel to the back of the head of the nearest man.

"Table's a mite messy already," Fargo said, "so a little more mess wouldn't make much of a difference. Now, what did Ike Sevier want with you fellas?"

The man nearest Fargo spoke first. "I do not know."

"That's not what I wanted to hear," Fargo said, thumbing back the hammer of the big Colt.

"Men," said a man across the table. "He was looking for men. We were not interested, because he could not pay us."

"What did he need men for?"

"Guns. He was going to steal guns."

"Who has the guns?"

"I do not know who has them. The man, Ike, was going to steal them. He said he had planned to buy them at first, but

58

he did not get the money as he had planned. Now he has to steal the guns."

"What does he want with guns?" Fargo asked.

"He did not say. Maybe to sell. He has no money. He said he would pay us if we got the guns. We do not believe in doing business that way. Especially Paco." The man looked at the floor. "Your friend Ike, he did not like Paco."

"He's not my friend," Fargo said.

"He was not Paco's friend, either, because Paco wanted to be paid before the guns were stolen and sold again."

The man's story wasn't complete, but what there was of it fit with what Fargo knew, especially the part about Ike not having gotten his hands on some money.

Fargo let down the hammer of the pistol, and the man in front of him sighed with relief.

"I hope you were telling the truth," Fargo said. "If you weren't, I'll come back here looking for you."

"You will not find me," the man said. "Or any of us."

Fargo figured that was the honest truth, but it didn't matter. He wouldn't have come back anyway. He turned and went to the door.

"You find out what you wanted to know?" Alvie said.

"I'm not sure," Fargo told him. "Maybe some of it. Let's get out of here."

"Glad to," Alvie said, and they walked out into the sunshine. "Your foot seems to be okay. Must not've been hurt as bad as I thought."

"I heal fast," Fargo said.

When he and Alvie had gone a little distance from Rosita's, Fargo looked back and said, "I wonder what that bartender's name really is."

"I don't know," Alvie said, "but I'm pretty sure it ain't Rosita."

5

As they walked back in the direction of the jail, Fargo told Alvie what the man had said about the guns.

"Guns mean the army," Alvie said.

Fargo thought the same thing. "Lots of army posts out west of here along the lower road to El Paso. Could be a shipment of guns going to one of them."

The forts were Lancaster, Clark, Inge, Stockton, and Davis. Most of them were fairly new, and they were supposed to protect travelers to El Paso and beyond against Apaches, Comanches, and Kiowas. It wasn't always an easy job because for many years the Indians had used that part of Texas as their raiding route into northern Mexico. They didn't take kindly to anyone else being in the way.

"Could be a shipment right here in town," Alvie said. "We can ask somebody."

"Might as well," Fargo said. "Maybe we can find somebody who knows more than we do."

"That oughta be easy," Alvie said.

They walked along St. Mary's Street just off the river until they came to a residential area. Alvie turned left, and soon they stopped in front of a large two-story house.

"This here used to be the Vance house," Alvie said. "Now it's the army headquarters."

"Seems like the Alamo would be better."

"They just use it for storage. Come on. I know the head honcho here."

They walked under some pecan trees and up on the porch of the building. A guard stood at the door.

"At ease, Private," Alvie said, showing the man his badge. "We need to talk to Colonel Bolton."

The soldier stepped aside without a word, and Alvie and Fargo entered the house.

"Office is right here," Alvie said, indicating an open door to what had once been a sitting room.

He tapped on the doorframe, and someone inside said, "Enter."

"Mornin', Colonel," Alvie said, stepping through the door. "This here fella's name is Fargo, and he's helpin' us out with some trouble. You heard about the marshal, I guess."

Colonel Bolton stood up behind his desk. He wasn't tall, but his military posture made him look taller than he was. He had a neatly trimmed mustache and thick black hair.

"I've heard," he said. "News travels fast in San Antonio, especially bad news. Marshal Benson was a good man." Bolton extended a hand across the desk to Fargo. "Pleased to meet you, Mr. Fargo. You're the one they call the Trailsman, I believe."

"That's me," Fargo said, shaking the colonel's hand.

"I've heard stories about you for a good many years. You've done a lot of work with the army."

"Sure have. Always a pleasure."

"No doubt. Well, have a seat, gentlemen, and tell me about this trouble and Marshal Benson's death. I'm curious to know how it affects me and my men."

Alvie and Fargo sat in a couple of wooden captain's chairs, and Fargo told as much of the story as he thought the colonel needed to know.

"Do you know what kind of guns?" Bolton asked when Fargo was finished.

"No. You know as much as I do."

"Could be Henry rifles, I suppose. They'd be worth a lot to the right people. Or to the wrong ones."

"Any stray Henrys around?"

"Not strays. There's a shipment on the way to Camp Hudson, but nobody's supposed to know about it."

Camp Hudson wasn't really even a fort, as evidenced by its name. It was located in the wild region on San Pedro Creek, not far from the Rio Grande. Fargo knew about it because that's where the Camel Corps had passed through. Fargo had been hired later on in the course of the camels' journey to help get them to California, and some of the men had mentioned Camp Hudson.

"That'd be just the kinda thing Ike Sevier'd be interested in," Alvie said. "Somethin' that'd make him good money. He'd sell the guns to Apaches without thinkin' twice. I'm not surprised he found out about the shipment. You know how hard it is to keep a secret in this town."

"Next to impossible," Bolton said.

"These rifles are for the soldiers at the camp?" Fargo asked.

"Do you know anything about the lower road between here and El Paso?" Bolton asked instead of answering.

"I've traveled it," Fargo said.

Bolton smiled. "Of course you have. You probably know more about it than I do."

"I doubt that, Colonel."

"No matter. You certainly know that any of the Indian tribes that roam that area of Texas would like to have some new Henry rifles for their raids into Mexico or their attacks on travelers and settlers, as Alvie mentioned."

Fargo noticed that the colonel hadn't answered his question, but he didn't press it.

"Be just like that damned Ike to sell 'em to the Injuns, all right," Alvie said. "Comanches, Apaches—it wouldn't bother him. He wouldn't give a damn about our own soldiers."

Bolton turned in his chair and looked out the window. He didn't say anything for a while. Fargo glanced at Alvie, who shrugged. Fargo didn't mind the wait. He got out his makin's and rolled a cigarette. He'd smoked it halfway down when Bolton turned back to them.

"There's a reason nobody is supposed to know about those guns," the colonel said. "Someone under my command has betrayed a trust, or your Mr. Sevier wouldn't know about them at all."

Fargo pinched out his quirly and slipped the remains in a pocket.

"I'm going to tell you something that might help you," Bolton said, "but it can go no further than this room."

Fargo thought it had already gone a lot farther than that, but he knew it wouldn't be wise to say so.

"We know how to keep quiet," Alvie said.

"I trust that you do."

Bolton looked out the window again. Fargo and Alvie waited.

"The rifles aren't for our soldiers," Bolton said, getting around to it at last. "They would be useful to them, in spite of their flaws, but they're for someone else."

Fargo had a Henry. He didn't mind the fact that the barrel could sometimes get a little too hot to hold or that the cartridges had to be loaded awkwardly. The repeating rifle's good points made up for its shortcomings as far as he was concerned.

"If the guns ain't for the soldiers, who're they for?" Alvie asked.

"Benito Juárez," Bolton said. "You know about him?"

"Got kind of a mess down there in Mexico," Fargo said. "He's on one side of it."

"That's close enough. The president doesn't openly support Juárez's revolution, but there are many reasons why we favor his side, and the McLane-Ocampo Treaty gives us some excuse to give a bit of help."

"I thought that treaty hadn't been ratified," Fargo said.

"That's true, which explains why we don't openly give our help. But we do what we can, and this shipment of guns was to be one way of aiding Juárez and his cause."

"And now Ike's gettin' in the way," Alvie said.

"The guns would be worth a good deal of money to interested parties," Bolton said.

Fargo was starting to get an idea of what was going on. He didn't think Ike was planning to buy the guns with the bank robbery money. More likely he was planning to pay off his informant, who might also be helping to transport the rifles. If that was the case, he'd have been expected to help Ike and his now-dead relatives steal the rifles from the army, too. Some of the money might even have gone to hire more men, but at the moment Ike was still on his own, and he didn't have the money to get anybody to help him.

It might not have been that way at all, though. Ike and his cousins wouldn't have needed to steal the guns, not with the money they got from the bank. That would have kept them happy for a good while. It wasn't worth worrying about. Ike was after the guns now. That was what mattered.

"The rifles were going to be handed over to Juárez at Camp Hudson?" Fargo said.

"To his representative. We don't know who that is, but arrangements have been made so that he'll be able to identify himself to the fort commander."

It didn't much matter who the representative was. He wouldn't be happy if the guns didn't show up as promised, and it wouldn't help the relationship between Mexico and the States if Juárez came out the winner down south.

"When did the guns leave San Antonio?" Fargo asked.

"Exactly one week ago."

If Ike had planned to catch up with the shipment on the road, it wasn't going to be easy. The wagon would be halfway to Camp Hudson by now, or even closer than that. Besides, there was no way Ike could ambush it without plenty of men. The shipment would be moving slow, though, and with some hard riding, Ike still might be able to get to Camp Hudson about the time it did. What he'd do then was anybody's guess, but somehow Fargo didn't think he'd just give up.

"What're you thinkin', Fargo?" Alvie asked.

"That I need to get on the road," Fargo said.

"You think that's what Ike'll do? Head for Camp Hudson and try to get the rifles?"

"Who knows? But if I get started now, I'll be ahead of him no matter what he decides."

"He might be on his way already," Alvie said.

"He needs men. He'll have to find them."

Fargo stood up, as did Alvie and the colonel.

"I wish I could offer you some help," Bolton said, "but the ones I could have spared are escorting the wagon with the rifles. We don't have any telegraph lines between here and the western posts, either. I could send a rider, but you might be just as fast as he would be."

"I expect you're right," Fargo said. He turned to go.

"Just a moment," Bolton said. "I'll write you an introduction to Major Wellman. He's the man in charge at Camp Hudson."

Bolton sat down, picked up a pen, and dipped it into an open bottle of ink. He scrawled something on a piece of official stationery, blotted it, folded it, and handed it to Fargo.

"That should do it. Wellman will give you whatever help he can. It won't be much because he's so shorthanded there, just as all the commanders are out west."

"I appreciate it," Fargo said, slipping the letter into his shirt.

He and Bolton shook hands again, and Fargo and Alvie left. When they were outside, Alvie said, "I noticed you didn't mention me going along with you."

"Troyce will be needing you here to help him run things," Fargo said.

"Troyce don't have what you'd call a high opinion of me. He's like the marshal, thinks moppin's all I'm good for. I guess you think that's about right, too."

"I saw you in Rosita's. You're a lawman, not a floor mopper."

"Thanks, Fargo. If you really believe that, you'll let me ride out with you. Maybe Troyce'll believe it, too, when we come back here with Ike."

"What if we don't come back?"

"You mean what if I don't. You always come back."

"So far."

"I'm willin' to take my chances with you if you'll have me. I can keep up, and I'll be a help. I know the country near 'bout well as you do, I'll bet. You see if I don't."

Fargo was used to working alone, but Alvie knew Ike and he might be of some help if he could keep up.

"You think you can stay with me?" he asked.

"Durned right. And if I can't, I'll turn back and mop some floors."

"All right," Fargo said. "You go tell Troyce. I'll meet you

66

at Fowler's livery in half an hour. If you're not there, I'll have to leave without you."

"I'll be there," Alvie said, "and I'll stick to you like a sticker burr up on a sandy-land hill."

Fargo laughed. "That sounds a mite too close."

"I'll keep my distance, then, but I'll be with you all the way. You'll see."

Fargo was afraid of that.

Ike Sevier cussed loud and long as he rode through the flat, dry land to the west of San Antonio. No one heard him. He was following the lower road, but he hadn't met anybody because not too many made the trip from west to east. Most everybody went the other way, looking to get out to California and get rich.

It was that damn Fargo who got Ike's goat and made him cuss. Three times now Fargo had stepped in where he wasn't wanted and messed up Ike's plans, first at the wagon train, then at the bank, and finally at the saloon.

Maybe the last time hadn't been so bad since Ike wasn't getting very far with those Mexicans, anyway. The nerve of those bastards, especially that mouthy one they'd called Paco, asking him for money up front like they didn't trust him, and him a white man.

Well, Ike had shown them, all right, shot the hell out of that damn Paco right there in front of all of them and nothing they could do about it but take it and like it. They'd have killed him if they could have, sure, but they had too much else to worry about and he'd got away from there before they had a chance at him. They'd taken it out on Fargo, but he figured the son of a bitch had got away. It would take more than a saloon full of Mexicans to kill a man like that.

He wondered if the Mexicans would come after him. He didn't think so. They were lazy and they didn't know where he'd gone. He might have told them enough so they could figure it out, but they were dumb as dirt. He didn't think he had anything to worry about from them.

That damn Fargo, though, he was a different story. How the hell had he known that Ike was in Rosita's in the first place? It was like the fella had some kind of spooky tracking sense. Maybe that's why they called him the Trailsman. Maybe the son of a bitch was even tracking Ike right now.

Ike wondered if any of the others had recognized Fargo in the bank. He sure as hell had. It was hard to forget that buckskin outfit. It was pure bad luck to run into him at the wagon train, but for him to turn up at the bank, well, that was even worse. It was spooky, all right.

Ike looked over his shoulder. If Fargo was tracking him, well, that was just fine with Ike, who was keeping a close eye on his back trail and who'd like nothing better than to get another chance at Fargo.

Not face-to-face, though. That would be taking too big a chance. A nice little back-shooting, that's what Fargo needed. It would do Fargo a world of good, not to speak of how much better it would make Ike feel to see the bastard squirming in the dust as he bled out. By God, he hoped Fargo *was* trailing him. He'd show him a thing or two.

That thought gave Ike so much satisfaction that he gave up on cussing Fargo and started to consider his situation with regard to the guns. He had the kind of information that was worth a lot of money, but what good was it doing him? He couldn't fight a military escort all on his own.

He knew Corporal Andy Chandler, but that was all, and he didn't know how much he could count on Chandler. After all, Chandler didn't even know Ike was coming after the guns.

He'd gotten drunk and told Ike about the guns one night in a bar, the night after the attempt on the wagon train.

Ike knew right then that those guns could make him and his cousins plenty of money, but his cousins wouldn't listen to him. After that mess at the wagon train, they'd come up with the plan to rob the bank. They told him it'd be a lot easier than taking guns from the army.

Ike hadn't been hard to convince. To do the bank job, they wouldn't even have to leave town, and they'd all have plenty of money for a good while. They could go to Galveston or even New Orleans and live the high life with women and whiskey.

But Fargo had come along and put the quietus on that idea. Now Ike was just about flat broke. He might've talked those Mexicans into helping him if he'd had a little more time, but Fargo had popped up again and ruined everything.

Ike wasn't going to let that stop him, however. He had more than one string for his bow. That was one thing about him. He never ran out of ideas. If one thing failed him, he'd try something else.

The wagon train business hadn't panned out, and the bank robbery hadn't worked, either. All right, then he'd hire some men and go after the army's guns.

Fargo had messed up that deal, too, and while Ike was plenty mad about it, he wasn't going to let it stop him. A plan was already half-formed in his mind, and he'd keep working it out as he rode along. It wasn't like he had anything else to do except keep his eyes open and watch for Fargo.

He'd already decided to kill Fargo. Now he just had to count on the Trailsman to come after him. And to find a good place for an ambush. The buzzards would be at Fargo's entrails before the damn Trailsman even knew what hit him.

* * *

Alvie put his hands on the saddle horn and pressed down. He raised himself up off the thinly padded saddle and stood with his feet planted firmly in the stirrups. After a couple of seconds he lowered himself, wiggled until he found the position he wanted, and said, "My hind end gets mighty tired after a while."

He and Fargo had been on the trail for about four days, and they hadn't seen any sign of Ike. They'd met only a couple of other people on the road, and they said they hadn't seen Ike, either.

"Everybody gets a little tired now and then," Fargo agreed. "Always feels good to get some air under you for a little while."

"You reckon Ike's really goin' after them guns?" Alvie said. "He could be in Galveston or Houston for all we know. He might not even want the guns."

"He seems to me like the kind that won't give up," Fargo said. He leaned over and patted the neck of his big Ovaro. "We'll be coming up to Fort Inge before night." Inge was about halfway to Camp Hudson. Fargo looked at the sinking sun. "That won't be long now. Maybe somebody there can tell us something."

"Maybe. Maybe not. I doubt Ike'd be stopping there, not if he thinks we're behind him."

"He might make a mistake," Fargo said.

"He's made a lot of 'em, all right. One more wouldn't surprise me." Alvie looked around. "If he is out here, you reckon he knows we're after him?"

Fargo couldn't answer that, but he suspected that Ike was being careful. So was Fargo, but it wasn't easy to track a man if you didn't know what kind of tracks he was making. About all Fargo could watch for was some place on the road where a rider had left the track and headed off into the sparsely timbered countryside. He'd seen a place like that a few miles back, but the ground was hard and dry and the tracks petered out on stony ground only a few yards away from the road. Fargo had been keeping a close watch ever since.

"If he knows we're after him," Alvie said, "he's bound to try to bushwhack us somewhere along the line. He caught the marshal off guard or he'd never have got him. He's likely to try to catch us the same way. Look over yonder. See that little hummock?"

Fargo saw it, all right. It was high enough to conceal both a man and a horse if they were lying down, and it was the only place within several miles that might serve Ike as an ambush point because the land was so flat and the vegetation so sparse. Rocks were scattered all around, some big, some small, but none of them large enough to hide a man, much less a horse.

Fargo had been looking at the hummock for several minutes now, trying to discern any movement that might indicate someone was lying low behind it, but so far he'd seen nothing.

Fargo scanned the countryside all around the hummock. While there didn't appear to be another place to hide, there was always a chance that Ike was out there somewhere, waiting for the right opportunity.

As if to confirm Fargo's intuition, a rifle cracked and a bullet ripped the hat right off Alvie's head. Alvie pulled back hard on the reins, then let go and fell backward as his horse reared and bumped Fargo's Ovaro, shoving it to the side just as another shot tore through the air right about where Fargo had been sitting.

Fargo rolled out of the saddle and behind the biggest rock he could find. It wasn't anywhere big enough to hide him.

The shots had come from somewhere in back of them. It was Ike, Fargo thought. Bound to be. Who else would try shooting him and Alvie in the back?

Fargo wondered how he could have missed seeing Ike's hiding place, but he didn't have time to worry about it. A bullet struck the ground to his left, digging a little trench in the dirt.

Fargo twisted himself around behind the rock and tried to make himself smaller. He didn't have much luck. He did, however, get a glimpse of Ike's head just before it disappeared below the level ground. Ike wasn't behind the hummock, after all. Must be a dry wash or gully back that way, and Ike was down in it. Fargo had missed seeing it or any sign of it, but then he hadn't been looking for anything like that. Fargo drew his Colt and waited for Ike to raise up again.

"You okay, Fargo?" Alvie asked.

"So far. You?"

"Lost my damn hat. Mighty good hat, too. Wish people'd stop messin' with it."

Fargo grinned in spite of himself. "You'll get it back."

"If Ike don't kill me first."

Fargo didn't turn around to look for Alvie, who must have been lying there with no cover at all, or maybe a rock about the size of a butter bean.

"He's not much of a shot," Fargo said.

"Lucky for us," Alvie said. "You got any idea where he's hidin'?"

"Nope."

"Me neither. What're we gonna do? We just gonna lie here?"

Fargo couldn't think of anything else to do. "You got a better idea?"

"Sure wish I could tell you I did. But I don't."

They lay there for a while without speaking. Several minutes dragged by with no sign of Ike.

"He don't want us to pick him off," Alvie said. "Ain't gonna show himself."

Alvie might be right, Fargo thought, but where could Ike go? He couldn't get out of the wash without being seen, not unless it was deeper than Fargo reckoned and not unless it ran for a long way. Ike could be moving along it, looking for a place where he could get a better shot, however. He might pop up anywhere along the bank. The problem was that Fargo couldn't tell where the bank was or even if it ran straight or made a curve or two. Nothing to do but wait and see what Ike did next.

Fargo could have waited a long time if he needed to, but it was getting close to sundown. It would be dark in an hour or so, and then things would change. Ike could wait, too.

"Old Ike, he's pretty smart," Alvie said. "He waited till we were pretty well past him to start shootin'. That pistol you got might not have the range to get him."

Fargo had already thought about that, but the Ovaro was standing too far away for Fargo to get to the Henry that was hanging in its sheath at the horse's side. He hoped Ike wouldn't think of shooting the horses.

Fargo heard a whir from behind a rock about five yards away. He knew what the sound was. He'd heard it before.

So did Alvie. "Rattlesnake. You see 'im?"

Fargo looked to his left. The snake slithered from behind the rock and coiled itself. Ike's second shot had probably stirred it up. Its head rose above the coil, and its eyes seemed to look straight at Fargo. The tip of its tail was a blur as it buzzed.

"I can see him," Fargo said.

"He don't like you much."

"I'm not real fond of him, either," Fargo said, but he didn't

73

mind the snake as long it kept its distance. He figured it would move along as sundown got closer, maybe return to its den, but at the moment the only thing that seemed to interest it was Fargo.

Its den would probably be nearby. Fargo hoped it was in the dry wash and that any other snakes from the den would locate Ike soon.

The snake uncoiled and moved a bit closer to Fargo, who didn't particularly want to kill it, though he would if it came any closer.

Fargo ignored the snake and looked toward the gully. The sun was so low now that it would be in Ike's eyes if he put his head over the edge. Maybe it had been in his eyes from the beginning. That could explain why he'd missed his first shot.

There was a chance that Fargo could run straight toward the wash and Ike wouldn't be able to see him well enough to hit him. Figure in the fact that Ike hadn't hit anybody so far, and it might be worth a try. Too bad the snake was in the way.

Too bad for the snake, that is. Fargo shot off its head as he rose to a crouch and started to run toward the dry wash.

Ike must have known what was happening, and he wasn't going to try shooting at a moving target that was facing him. He had one more trick in him. Fargo heard a shout and a shot. Ike's horse scrambled up from where it had lain under the rim of the gully and started to run.

The gully ran perpendicular to the road, and the horse was headed off to Fargo's left.

Fargo could see only the top half of the horse, mainly the head, hindquarters, and saddle. The rest of the animal was hidden by the lip of the wash, and Ike was nowhere to be seen. Fargo kept going, waiting for Ike to make a move.

When the horse came out of the gully, it was well out of pistol range, and that was when Ike swung himself into the saddle. He'd been hanging down on the off side. He rode low in the saddle, leaning forward on the horse's neck and hardly presenting a target at all. He was a better rider than he was a shooter.

Fargo heard the boom of a rifle behind him. Alvie had tried a shot, but the bullet didn't hit anything that Fargo could see. Alvie wasn't a much better shot than Ike. Maybe worse.

Fargo watched until Ike was out of sight, then turned and walked back to Alvie, who was standing beside his horse, a little pinto.

"Missed him," Alvie said. "Gettin' dusky dark. Hard to see."

"Were you aiming at the horse or the rider?"

Alvie looked hurt. He picked up his hat and slapped the dust out of it on his pants. When he had it sitting on his head just right, he said, "Wouldn't want to kill a horse if I didn't have to."

Fargo nodded. "Don't blame you. Not the best time of day for shooting at a small target, though."

The Ovaro was standing a few yards away. Fargo went over to him and picked up the reins.

"You reckon Ike'll stop at the fort?" Alvie said as they swung up into their saddles.

"I doubt it," Fargo said.

Ike was cursing Fargo as he rode. The Trailsman had spoiled his plans again. Instead of lying dead on the trail the way Ike had figured it out, he was just fine, maybe a little dirty from rolling off his horse, but that was all.

It was the damn sun, that's what it was, Ike thought. It was just his luck that the only cover he could find was in a spot where the sun would be in his eyes. He'd have hit the bastard otherwise.

Sure, he could have tried for Fargo when the sun would have been in the Trailsman's eyes, but that would have meant facing him head-on. That wasn't Ike's style, however, and he didn't dwell on it.

None of that mattered, anyhow. Ike had already formed another plan. It would take Fargo a little time to get mounted up and on the road again, and by that time Ike would be well ahead of him. Ike was sure Fargo wouldn't believe Ike would go to the fort, so that's exactly where he'd go.

And when he got there, he'd fix a little surprise for that damn Skye Fargo.

6

Fort Inge wasn't much to look at in the daylight, but it looked a little better in the early-evening dark. It consisted of a couple of barracks for the soldiers stationed there, an officers' quarters, and eight or ten other buildings surrounding the parade ground, the biggest being a large limestone structure used for a storehouse and commissary. A stable stood at the south end of the fort. All the buildings other than the commissary were built of thin, upright poles plastered with mud and grass.

A big early-rising full moon gave the whitewashed buildings an eerie glow as Ike rode up to them. He was stopped by a picket guard who then let him pass by without giving him any trouble. Ike looked more like a kid running away from home to seek his fortune in California than a killer.

As soon as Ike was inside the fort, he tied his horse to a hitch rail and asked a nearby private to take him to the commanding officer. He was shown into a room in a building near the barracks, where a captain in uniform sat at a desk reading some papers by lamplight.

"This man asked to see you, sir," the private said after saluting.

The captain dismissed the trooper and said, "I'm Captain Salter. What do you want?"

Salter had bright black eyes, thick black hair, and a stony face. He looked to Ike to be the kind of man who didn't care to hear any unnecessary details, so Ike started right in with his story.

"Some men tried to kill me a few miles back down the road toward San Antonio," he said. "I was riding along, not watching my back like I should've been, because I'm too trusting, I guess, and they bushwhacked me."

Ike described the location where he'd made his own attack and described Fargo and Alvie as the men who'd tried to kill him. He explained that he'd managed to escape because the two were poor shots and he had a faster horse than they did.

"I think they wanted my money," Ike finished. "They're dangerous men. Desperate, you might say."

"What does all this have to do with me?" Salter asked. "I'm not the law."

"You're the law on this post," Ike said. "If they show up here, you'd better lock them in the guardhouse before they rob somebody or kill them."

The captain looked Ike over. What he saw was a smooth-faced young man who looked as if he'd never told a lie in his life. The captain brushed his clipped mustache and asked Ike if he'd ever seen the men before.

"In San Antonio. They were at the livery stable when I got my horse. I'm on the way to El Paso with some money my daddy needs for a land deal, and they might've heard me mention that to the owner." Ike looked at the floor. "I should have kept quiet. My daddy always told me to keep my mouth shut about things like that, but I can't seem to remember."

"Well, you have nothing to worry about here," the captain said. He stood up. "I'll see to it that you're well taken care of and that those two miscreants are dealt with properly if they try anything."

"Thanks," Ike said. "That's a mighty generous offer, but I

can't stay here. If I don't get the money to El Paso on time, my father won't be able to close that land deal he's been working on. I'll have to ride right through most of the night and all day tomorrow before I rest up again."

The captain looked doubtful. "That's mighty hard riding. Are you sure your horse is up to it? Are you sure *you're* up to it?"

"I have to be, sir. My father's counting on me. I can't let him down."

"That's a commendable attitude, son, and I admire a man who knows his duty and sticks to it. But what if those men come after you?"

"They're more likely to stop here for something to eat and to get some rest. They probably think they've scared me so bad I won't stop running for a week."

"That might be, but what if you're wrong?"

"I'm way ahead of them now. They won't catch me."

Captain Salter looked doubtful. "Let me at least feed you a meal before you leave."

"I sure wish I could spare the time," Ike said, "but I need to get on the road right now. I just wanted to warn you about those two. They're hard men, back-shooters."

The conversation went on for a minute or two, with the captain trying to persuade Ike to rest and eat and Ike insisting that he had to be on the move. The captain gave in, and Ike left, thanking him again for his offer.

He got on his horse, hoping the animal was rested enough to go at least a few more miles before they stopped for the night. Ike would sleep out under the stars, while Fargo and his fuzzy-faced deputy friend slept in the guardhouse. With any luck, they'd be there for days. Ike grinned and turned the horse's head to the west.

* * *

Fargo and Alvie rode up to the fort about half an hour after Ike had gone on his way. The picket on the road didn't let them pass as he had Ike. Instead he said, "Follow me. I'll see you into the fort."

The fort was open, with no walls around it, so Fargo thought it was a little unusual for the guard to escort them, but he didn't say anything.

As they rode into the parade ground that was partially enclosed by the buildings, they were joined by three other soldiers on horseback who fell in behind them. The men were burly and unsmiling types who looked as if they'd been through a tussle or two, considering that two of them had noses that had been broken more than once.

"Quite a welcome you fellas are givin' us," Alvie said. "You treat ever'body this-a-way?"

"We just want to be sure you're comfortable here," the guard said, not sounding like he meant it.

He came to a stop in front of a small building that appeared to be a bit sturdier than the others on the post. He dismounted and said, "The captain would like to meet you. He's inside."

Fargo didn't much like the setup, but he slid off the Ovaro as Alvie climbed off the pinto. The three soldiers behind them dismounted as well.

The guard walked up to the door and stood aside. "After you, gentlemen."

"Been a long time since anybody called me a gentleman," Alvie said, stopping on the narrow porch outside the building. "It's nice to meet a young fella with some respect for his elders."

"Just get inside," the guard said. His voice was harsh.

"Here, now, there ain't no need to take that tone with me, and me just sayin' how nice you were."

Fargo stopped just behind Alvie. "I don't think we need to meet your captain tonight," he said to the guard. "We're both tired and hungry. Just show us a place where we can rub down our horses and feed them. No need to bother with finding us a place to sleep. We'll bunk outside."

"You'll do what Private Patterson says," came a voice from behind Fargo. "You'll get inside, and you'll do it right now."

"Damned if I will," Alvie said. "I ain't in the army. You can't give no orders to me."

"Or to me," Fargo said.

He turned to face the men behind him. They'd put themselves between him and the horses. They looked as if they hoped Fargo would give them some trouble because they wanted to return it to him with interest.

"What the hell?" he heard Alvie say. "This here's the guardhouse. You gonna try to lock us up? What the hell's goin' on here, anyhow?"

Fargo heard scuffling and figured the picket was trying to get Alvie through the door. Fargo didn't turn around. He didn't take his eyes off the three men who were watching him.

"I think you have the wrong idea about me and my friend," he said. "Just let me get to my horse, and I'll show you something to change your minds."

The letter Colonel Bolton had written was in Fargo's saddlebags, where he'd put it before leaving San Antonio.

"You just stay put right where you are," the man in the middle said. He was the biggest of the three, a sergeant, likely the fort commander's enforcer. He looked as if he hoped Fargo wouldn't stay put.

The scuffle behind Fargo grew more intense, so he turned to see what was happening. Alvie had his hands braced on either side of the doorframe and the guard tried to push him inside. The guard had a pistol in one hand, and he jammed it in Alvie's kidney. Alvie went through the door. Fargo took a step toward them, and a big hand landed on his shoulder.

Fargo wasn't a small man by any means, but the sergeant turned him around without straining.

"I told you to stay put," the sergeant said. "You should've listened."

Fargo expected the man to swing at him, but it didn't happen like that. Instead, he squeezed Fargo's shoulder so hard that it felt as if it were on fire. The other two soldiers jumped forward and made a grab for Fargo's arms.

Fargo swung weakly at them, but they weren't much affected. They took hold of his arms, and the third man relaxed his grip a little. Fargo heard Alvie yell behind him.

"Don't let 'em get you, Fargo."

Too late for that, Fargo thought as the men on either side of him stretched out his arms and pulled so hard that Fargo thought the arms might pop right off.

"Hold him tight," the sergeant said.

He released Fargo's shoulder, which was a relief, but the relief lasted only until the man hit Fargo in the stomach with a fist the size of a bucket.

Fargo took it as well as anybody could have, which was a lot better than most. It didn't seem to make the big man happy that he hadn't cried out, so he hit Fargo again. Fargo wanted to double over, but the two men holding him had other ideas. They kept him upright, and the soldier began to hit him steadily, keeping his blows right around the same spot every time.

"There's . . . a . . . letter . . ." Fargo said.

"Yeah, in your saddlebags." The sergeant hit Fargo again. And again.

Fargo wondered how many more blows he could take. He was pretty sure he couldn't last until the man got tired of hitting him. Luckily, he didn't have to. The two men released his arms, and Fargo slumped. He didn't go to his knees, though. He wasn't going to give the man that satisfaction.

"Kelly," the man said.

There was movement on Fargo's left. He started to turn his head to see what was happening, but it was as if his neck wouldn't cooperate. The shoulder squeeze had just about paralyzed him. He hardly had time to wonder if he'd ever be able to turn his head again when something hard smashed into it, sending him reeling.

He was unconscious before he hit the ground.

"You awake, Fargo?" Alvie asked.

Fargo stirred on the straw mattress where he lay.

"I guess I am. Where are we?"

"The guardhouse," Alvie said. He sat on the side of a bunk just like the one where Fargo lay. "How're you feelin'?"

"I've felt better," Fargo said.

He looked up at the light coming through the small barred window near the top of the wall beside his bunk.

"Daylight. I must have slept pretty good."

"Must have. I didn't hear you snore or anything. You even missed reveille."

Fargo didn't think that was any great loss. He considered sitting up. It didn't seem like a good idea, but he gave it a try. It wasn't as bad as he'd thought it might be, though it made his head throb and his shoulder twinge. His stomach felt as if he'd been kicked by a mule with a serious grudge against him.

"Those fellas didn't give us a fair chance," Alvie said. "If they had, we could'a whipped their asses for 'em like we did back at Rosita's."

Fargo wasn't so sure of that. "Is there any water in here?"

"Just a slops bucket," Alvie said. "You wouldn't want to drink from that. Anyhow, you don't need to. Reason I woke you up is that the captain here sends his apologies and wants us to have breakfast with him."

"You must have been dreaming," Fargo said.

"Nope. Soldier boy came in here while you were sleepin' and told me so."

"Why the welcome, then?"

"Can't tell you anything about that. Maybe the captain can. All I know is, I'm glad to be gettin' out of this place. I think I got fleas from this mattress. They don't wash the blankets real regular, either."

"Reckon there's a place around here where we can wash up?"

"Now that hurts my feelin's," Alvie said. "Here I've already got myself cleaner'n a whistle, and you didn't even notice it."

"Sorry. Where'd you get a bath?"

"Didn't say I got a bath. There's a pump and a horse trough, though."

"That'll do," Fargo said.

He steadied himself with both hands on the side of the bunk, took a breath, and stood up.

"That wasn't so bad, now, was it?" Alvie said.

"Could be worse. Show me that pump and horse trough."

"Let me look you over, first."

Alvie stood up and stepped over to Fargo. He looked at the side of Fargo's head and let out a low whistle.

"That's some knot. Big as an apple. Skin's not broke, though. That's good."

Fargo reached up and touched the spot on his head where he'd been hit. Alvie had exaggerated the size of the knot, but not by a lot. It was as big as a good-sized egg.

"You must have a damn hard head," Alvie said.

"So I've been told. Let's go get cleaned up."

"You sure you can walk?"

"I'm sure," Fargo said, though he wasn't sure at all. But it turned out that he could.

Captain Salter had laid out a breakfast in his quarters. Scrambled eggs, ham, biscuits, gravy, and hot coffee. Fargo hadn't eaten that well in a good while.

"I'm sorry about the reception we gave you two," Salter said as Fargo and Alvie ate. "Particularly you, Mr. Fargo. It was a mistake on my part."

"Just Fargo is fine."

"Fargo, then. It was a bad blunder."

"Sure as hell was," Alvie said, his mouth full of biscuit. "What I'd like to know is why you let us go."

Fargo wanted to know that, too, but he was more interested in why they'd been beaten and locked up in the first place. He figured Salter would get around to telling them eventually.

"I let you go because one of my men finally got around to mentioning that you said something about a letter in your saddlebags. I sent someone to check, and he found it. Excuse me, and I'll get it and return it to you."

He left the room.

"Sure do wish he'd looked for that letter last night," Alvie said. "I bet you do, too."

"You'd win that bet," Fargo said.

Salter came back with the letter as Fargo was shoveling in the last bite of his ham and eggs. The officer waited until Fargo was through chewing and handed the letter to him.

"Colonel Bolton wouldn't have given you this if he didn't trust you. I hope you don't mind my reading it."

"I'm glad you did," Fargo said.

"Should've read it sooner," Alvie said.

"Again, my apologies to both of you. I was taken in by someone. At my age, I should know better than to put much faith in appearances, but he fooled me completely."

"That damn Ike Sevier," Alvie said.

"Looks like he hasn't started to shave yet? Has a glib way about him?"

"He can talk a man into a lot of things," Alvie said. "He talked the marshal in San Antonio plumb to death."

"Benson? He's dead?"

"That man you talked to last night's Ike Sevier," Alvie said. "He killed him."

Salter was silent for a while. "I knew he was a liar because of that letter, and now you tell me he's a killer, as well."

"Looks like a mama's boy," Alvie said, "but he ain't."

"Far from it, it seems."

"That's not all," Fargo said. He told Salter about the guns.

"Good God. That shipment came through here only a few days ago. It's heavily guarded. Surely this man can't be planning to steal the guns. One man wouldn't stand a chance."

"I wouldn't try to predict what he might do," Fargo said. "I didn't think he'd show his face here, but he did." He touched the knot on his head, which seemed a little smaller now. "He set us up good, too."

"I supposed you're going after him," Salter said. "I've delayed you so much that you might not be able to catch up."

"We'll have to try," Fargo said.

"You're in no condition to do much riding."

"I hope you ain't talkin' to me," Alvie said.

"No. I'm sure you're in fine fettle. You didn't get the same treatment Fargo did."

Alvie reached around and felt his back. "You ain't seen my kidney."

Salter looked pained. "I've spoken to all four men involved. They believed they were doing their duty and following my orders. I admit I didn't think they'd have to resort to such harsh measures."

"I hope I don't run into any of 'em again," Alvie said. "I don't know as I could control my gun hand."

Fargo lowered his head so that Alvie and Salter couldn't see his grin.

"Do you also hold a grudge, Fargo?" Salter asked.

"There's a sergeant I wouldn't mind having a word or two with."

"I can have him apologize to you personally if that would help."

"Wouldn't make me feel a lot better." Fargo pushed back from the table and stood up. "I thank you for the breakfast, but now me and Alvie had better be on our way."

"I had the men take care of your horses last night," Salter said. "They'll be in better shape than Ike Sevier's."

"I appreciate that, too," Fargo said.

He put out his hand, and Salter took it. They shook, and Fargo said, "No hard feelings. I can see why you did what you did."

"Me, too," Alvie said. "You gonna send anybody along with us to help us out?"

"I wish I could, but my men are needed for patrol here. Unless this Sevier is smarter than I think he is, you'll be more than a match for him."

"You done misjudged him once," Alvie said. "It'd be a worse mistake to do it twice."

"You're right," Salter said, "but I still can't spare the men. We're shorthanded as it is."

"We thank you anyway for the breakfast," Fargo said.

"Our hospitality was poor otherwise, I'm afraid. If you come back this way, we'll do better by you."

"If Ike comes back, I hope you do worse by him," Alvie said.

"I can promise you that," Salter said.

Ike pushed his horse too hard and had to rest it often. That slowed him down. He was afraid that Fargo and Alvie would come along before he caught up with the wagon, but they didn't.

When he saw the dust of the wagon and its escort in the distance, he rode off the trail and thought about what he was going to do. He'd have to talk to Andy Chandler and convince him to help steal the guns. There was a way to do that. There had to be. All Chandler would have to do was make sure the wagon was unguarded at night after Ike gave him the word. But there were plenty of problems.

Ike didn't have any men to help him, and he could have used plenty of help.

He didn't have any contact with the Comanches, either, not that he wanted any. He'd deal with them through others, and he had a way of doing that if things worked out. Back when he broached his plan about the guns, his cousins had said they knew some men who traded with the Indians, and they'd told Ike that those men would be more than happy to pay a decent price for the rifles because they could get even more from the Indians.

That was all true, or Ike thought it was. His cousins didn't lie to him about things like that, though they'd lied to him about plenty of other things over the years. They'd even told him in a general way how to find the traders, who were located not too far from Camp Hudson.

Ike didn't know the men or how he'd be received, however, and that was a little worrisome. His cousins had seemed afraid of them, and they weren't afraid of very much. That was one of the reasons they'd preferred to make a try at the wagon train and then do the bank job. Too bad those things hadn't worked out for them.

Even if Ike couldn't find the traders, there were other ways to get money for the rifles. Ike had thought of a few of them, but he'd have to work all that out later. First, he had to get the guns. And keep them.

Considering the difficulties involved, most men would have given up and decided that making an honest living would be a lot easier. Ike didn't think that way. He'd never made an honest living in his life, and he didn't know anybody who had. Being around his cousins for most of his life, he'd picked up the idea that working an honest job was something you did if you weren't smart enough for anything else.

Ike, who'd always thought he was smarter than just about anybody else, got off the road but followed its route as closely as he could. There was plenty of cover here, and he didn't worry about being spotted. They were getting into the Trans-Pecos region of Texas, down near the Mexican border, and the terrain sprouted rocks and bushes in about equal measure. Hills, low mesquite trees, brush, and ocotillo cactus dotted the landscape.

Late in the afternoon, Ike got close enough to the road to see that one of the men escorting the wagons was hanging back a bit from the others. The rear guard. Ike thought he recognized the man, so he rode closer to get a better look, and sure enough, the man was Andy Chandler.

Ike dismounted, picked up a small rock, and got back on his horse. He rode along behind some mesquites until he had a clear shot. He tossed the rock softly, and it hit Chandler on the shoulder.

The corporal turned, rifle in hand, and looked into the brush. Ike showed himself, holding his hands up, palms outward.

Chandler gave a little nod, showing that he recognized Ike, and rode forward. He spoke briefly to another soldier before riding off into the brush, where Ike met him.

"I told 'em I was gonna take a piss," Chandler said. "What the hell are you doing here?"

"What do you mean? You know what I'm doing here."

"The hell you say. I'm not even sure who you are."

Ike shook his head and gave Chandler a grin. "You know, all right. I'm the man you told about these guns."

Chandler gave his head a rueful shake. "I knew that was a big mistake. I shouldn't've done it. I'd been drinking a little."

"You'd been drinking a lot," Ike said. "I guess you don't even remember promising to help me steal the guns."

Chandler gaped at him. "I never said a thing like that. You must be crazy. I'm going back out there, and you can get away from here."

"You wouldn't want me to do that. I might just go to Camp Hudson and tell them about the man I met in a bar and the shipment of guns he mentioned."

"You wouldn't do that."

Ike gave him a grin. "Sure I would. I'd hate to see you locked up in the guardhouse for a month or two, but I'd do it, right enough."

"Bastard."

"Could be. I never asked my mama about that."

"I can't do it."

"You don't have to do much. Just make sure the wagon's not guarded tonight. I'll do the rest."

Chandler considered it. "How can I make sure the wagon's not guarded?"

"That part's up to you," Ike told him. "If you want to come in on this deal with me, I can promise you some money. If you don't come in with me, that's fine, too. I don't care. Just make sure nobody's with that wagon tonight. You won't be blamed for what happens. I'll make sure of that."

"Sergeant Sullivan keeps two men with the wagon all the time. I can't get rid of them."

"Just two men?"

"That's all."

That was good news for Ike. "Hell, you and I can take care of two men. You get rid of one of them, and I'll take the other one."

"I'm not killing anybody, no matter what you threaten me with."

"I didn't say you had to kill him. Just keep him quiet. Hit him in the head and drag him off somewhere. That's good enough."

"If I was on duty, it'd be easier. I'd let you hit me, and then you could worry about the other one."

Ike liked the sound of that idea. "Trade duty with somebody tonight. Can you do that?"

Again, Chandler had to consider it. "Maybe. One of the men owes me a favor. If I do trade off with him, I'll make sure I'm the one in back of the wagon. There'll be somebody in the front, too, sitting up in the seat. More'n likely he'll be asleep."

It was sounding too easy to Ike, but sometimes things worked out like that. It was about damn time, too. He'd had a run of bad luck lately, and he deserved for things to go his way for a change. It just proved that if you had a little gumption and kept on going, you'd come out ahead sooner or later. All you had to do was have a plan, even if it wasn't a very good one.

"Just keep quiet and let me take care of the man in the wagon," he said.

"You won't kill him?"

"Hell, no. Just give him a good knock in the head."

"I hate for anybody to get hurt."

"Damn it to hell. Can you do it, or can't you?"

"I can do it, I guess," Chandler said. "You come in about an hour before sunup. Everybody should be sleeping hard about then."

"I'll be there," Ike said.

"Even if everybody's asleep, I don't see how you think you can get that wagon away from here," Chandler said. "The mules won't be hitched to it. You'll have to do it, and if you manage that, you'll wake everybody up. And if you get away after all that, the escort'll catch you before you got half a mile."

Ike wished Chandler would just shut up. He sounded like Ike's cousins, always bringing up objections to Ike's plans but never coming up with anything better. They *thought* what they wanted to do was better, but the wagon train idea and the bank idea hadn't been worth a damn. Ike was going to make his plan work, one way or the other, even if it wasn't as easy as it had seemed only a minute earlier.

"You let me worry about all that," Ike said. "You just be where you're supposed to be."

"I'll be there," Chandler said, and he left to rejoin the escort.

Ike watched him go. He was pretty sure Chandler wouldn't be of much help to him. All the corporal could do was tell Ike why his plan wouldn't work. Ike needed help, not criticism, but he'd work something out.

He always did.

Ike didn't sleep much that night, but he rested as best he could. His mind was going a mile a minute to come up with a plan for getting the wagon. He finally thought of something he believed might work, and when he guessed it was about an hour before the sun would be coming up, he slipped to the edge of the soldiers' camp.

He could see the outlines of men in sleeping bags, and he could hear some of them snoring. The early-morning air had a chill in it, and nobody was stirring around, not even the cook, who would be up early to fix breakfast. Ike stood still to look over the camp. He located the horses and saw the long-eared mules with them. They were in a little rope corral not too far from the wagon, which was good news for Ike.

Ike had armed himself well. He had a pistol in a holster and a second one stuck in his belt. He had a bowie knife in a sheath that hung near the pistol.

A man, Chandler, Ike supposed, leaned against the side of the wagon near the back. Another sat in the seat, slumped over as if he was asleep.

Ike drifted around the edge of the camp quiet as a mist. He went up to the wagon and touched Chandler on the shoulder. The corporal twitched, but he didn't cry out.

"Get the mules over here," Ike said, his mouth beside Chandler's ear. "Don't make a sound."

For a second, he didn't think the soldier would do it, but then Chandler gave a slight nod and moved off.

Ike watched him for a second before going to the front of the wagon. When he climbed up to the seat, his weight made the wagon sag. The guard sat up and turned his head toward him, still half asleep.

Ike put a finger to his lips. The guard, not sure what was happening, didn't speak, and then Ike was beside him.

The guard sat up straighter and opened his mouth to yell for help, but Ike wrapped his arm around his head, covering his mouth with his hand.

In his other hand, Ike had the sharp bowie knife, and he slit the guard's throat without giving it a second thought, the way you'd butcher an animal. He didn't mind the blood that spurted over his hand. He hardly noticed it. He laid the soldier down in the floor of the wagon, wiped his knife and hands on the man's uniform, and climbed down.

Chandler came back with the mules only a few seconds later. Ike didn't know how he'd managed to get them away from the horses so quietly, and he didn't ask. He put his mouth near Chandler's ear and said, "Let's hook 'em up."

Somehow they managed it without waking the camp, though the harness had jangled a time or two. Chandler didn't mention the soldier who'd been in the wagon.

When they were finished, Ike beckoned Chandler closer and when the corporal bent down to hear what Ike had to say, Ike gave him the same surprise he'd given the other soldier. Ike's plan no longer included Chandler.

Chandler, being more alert than the sleeping soldier had been, struggled. It didn't help. Ike might have looked like a kid, but he had a grip like iron.

Chandler's heels kicked against the hard ground. He gurgled when he died.

Ike smiled as he cleaned his knife and stuck it in the sheath on his belt. He'd kept his promise. Chandler wouldn't be blamed for what was about to happen.

Some of the other men were beginning to stir, and before long the camp would be awake. Ike was going to help them along. He put his knife away and pulled the pistol from his holster and the second pistol from his belt.

He looked over the camp once more, took a deep breath, and ran. As he ran, he screamed and fired the pistols. Some shots hit the men sleeping on the ground. Others sent bullets whipping over the heads of the horses. The horses snorted, stamped their hooves, reared, and jumped. It took them only a couple of seconds to knock down their flimsy rope corral.

They ran blindly through the camp, trampling a couple of men who hadn't managed to untangle themselves from their blankets.

Avoiding the stampeding horses, Ike doubled back to the wagon. The confused mules were about to run after the horses, but Ike jumped into the wagon and lashed the mules with the reins. The animals jumped forward and pulled Ike and the wagon out of the camp.

One or two of the soldiers figured out what was happening and fired shots after Ike, but he was soon out of range.

Ike laughed aloud. He had the guns. Now all he had to do was locate the traders and sell the guns to them.

His plan had worked.

7

Fargo and Alvie rode into the soldiers' camp a couple of hours after sunrise. The horses, or most of them anyway, had been rounded up, but things were still in disarray.

Fargo located the sergeant, explained what he and Alvie were there for, and showed him the letter from Bolton.

"What happened here?" Fargo asked when the sergeant handed the letter back to him.

"Damned if I know," the sergeant said. His name was Burns, and he was nearly as big as the one who'd beaten Fargo at Fort Inge. "It was mighty confusing. All I know for sure is I have five dead men, two of 'em shot, two of 'em knifed, and one of 'em trampled. I got a burial detail taking care of them. And the wagonload of rifles is missing." He shook his head. "If I'm lucky they'll just break me back to private instead of cashiering me. Or having me shot."

Alvie looked around and said to Fargo, "You think Ike could'a done all this?"

"One man?" Burns said. "You think one man did this and got off with the guns, too?"

"Could be," Fargo said. "He's a mean son of a bitch. Might have been others with him, though. I'll take a look around."

It took Fargo about ten minutes to find where Ike's horse had been tied to a mesquite a half mile from the camp. There were signs that the wagon had passed that way, so Ike had the horse and the wagon now.

"One man," Fargo told Burns when he got back to camp. "He's headed off into the open country."

"One man," Burns said. "They're probably building a gallows for me already." He shook his head. "Soon's we get my men buried, we'll go after the bastard. You want to go with us?"

"Alvie and I will go on right now," Fargo said. "It's just one man."

"Yeah, and look what he did to me and my men."

"He's not so good at things like that when you're awake," Fargo said.

As they rode out of the camp, Alvie asked, "What d'you think Ike's got in mind, Fargo?"

Fargo looked down at the tracks of the wagon. "The way he's headed, I'd say he's looking for somebody to buy those guns."

"Who'd do that? Apaches? Comanches? They wouldn't buy any guns from Ike. They'd just kill him and take them."

"Ike might not think that way," Fargo said. "Or he might have somebody else in mind. Traders, maybe."

"Traders?" Alvie said. "You mean Comancheros? I'd as soon deal with a snake as with one of them fellas. Much less a whole bunch of 'em."

"Some of them are harmless," Fargo said.

Alvie leaned over and spat on the ground. "Ain't nobody who trades with the Comanches harmless."

Fargo knew that Alvie was wrong. Some of the traders in western Texas and New Mexico were peaceable enough, as were the Comanches they dealt with. The traders exchanged things like tools and tobacco for hides and horses. But there were other traders who were more sinister, dealing in whis-key and guns, if they could get them, and trading for slaves the Comanches had taken from other tribes. Fargo didn't know which kind of group Ike might be headed for, but he had a pretty good idea.

"You think we can stop him?" Alvie said.

"We can try," Fargo said.

The first thing Ike had to do was hide the guns. He'd already considered the fact that the men he was looking for might not be exactly of the finest sort.

Ike had a plan for that, of course. He always had a plan. The country he was in now was rocky and the beginnings of the West Texas mountain ranges were all around. As he drove the wagon, he looked for places he could make use of and found one soon enough—a place where the side of a hill had caved in sometime in the distant past. The opening wasn't large, but there was enough room for him to back the wagon in.

The mules didn't want to cooperate at first, but Ike coaxed them and finally got the job done. The entrance to the cave-in was partially concealed by brush, and large rocks all around helped to conceal the entrance from a distance.

Ike unhitched the mules and gathered enough brush to com-plete the job of hiding the wagon. The brush wouldn't fool any-body who was really looking, but nobody was likely to come that way because Ike had been lucky enough to find a way to go where the ground was so hard the wagon and mules weren't leaving any tracks at all. Some of the ground he'd passed over wasn't even ground at all, just solid rock.

Ike knew the soldiers would be after him, and probably that damned Fargo, too, but he didn't think they could track him. The scrub and brush would hide him from a distance, and he wasn't even kicking up any dust. He led the mules away from the hiding place. Things were going just the way he'd planned.

By noon it was obvious to Fargo that he wasn't going to find Ike. The wagon tracks had disappeared on the hard-packed ground, and before long there were no marks at all. He wasn't even sure in which direction Ike was traveling.

"He might be watching us from one of them hills," Alvie said, pointing off to the west. "Laughin' at us for lookin' like fools."

"I don't think so," Fargo said. "He's gone off somewhere, looking for somebody to sell those guns to."

"Reckon he'll find 'em?"

"If he does, I hope they give him a hot reception."

"Me, too," Alvie said. "You think it was just Alvie by himself that stole them guns? It don't seem likely that one man could've done all that damage."

"If he had any help, it's somebody we don't know about. Nobody was with him when he took those shots at us."

"For a fella that looks like a damn preacher's son, he sure can do a lot of damage."

"Even a rattlesnake looks harmless enough if you don't know what's on its mind," Fargo said.

"I guess that's the truth. You can't ever tell what's inside a man until you put him to the test. Ike'd fail just about ever' test there is. He's one sorry son of a bitch."

"I'd have to agree with you on that," Fargo said.

Alvie nodded. "Just about anybody'd have to agree. What're we gonna do now?"

Fargo couldn't see but one answer. "Go to Camp Hudson and see if Ike's there."

"You don't think he is, do you?"

"Not for a minute," Fargo said.

Someone else was at Camp Hudson, however—a group of ten Mexican troops sent by Benito Juárez. Nine of them were pretty much what Fargo would have expected: hard-looking men, not wearing any kind of uniforms but instead clad in dusty clothes and sombreros. They were heavily armed, not disciplined soldiers, but the kind of men who would have to be kept under tight control by their leader.

It was their leader who provided Fargo with a surprise.

"My name," she said, "is Adelita Guerrero Cruz, and I want to know what you have done with my rifles."

She was tall, almost as tall as Fargo, with black hair and black eyes that flashed with revolutionary fervor when she looked at Fargo. Or perhaps it was some other kind of fervor, the kind that Fargo was likely to enjoy a lot more. He hoped that was it, and he hoped he'd get the chance to find out.

Although Adelita wore men's clothing, there was no concealing the fact that she was a woman of spectacular dimensions. She had high, Indian cheekbones, a finely molded nose, and full, curved lips. Her clothes, unlike those of the men she led, were not dusty. She wore a pistol positioned for a cross-handed draw on her left hip, and a coiled leather bullwhip was clipped to her belt on the right. Fargo wondered if that was how she kept the men under control.

"I haven't done a thing with the rifles," Fargo said. "I didn't even know they were yours. I thought they were for Benito Juárez."

"You have no right to speak to me like this!" Adelita said. "I am the representative of Benito Juárez, and as such I should be treated with respect!"

"No disrespect meant," Fargo said.

They were in the office of Major Wellman. Wellman stood at his desk, looking amused at the confrontation that was taking place before him. Alvie stood off to the side, looking equally amused.

"I am a soldier as much as any man here," Adelita said. "I have proved myself in battle, and my men will tell you that I am the equal of any other. Better than most."

She gave Fargo a hard, challenging look when she said the last words, and he had to grin.

"I don't doubt it," he said. "I'm not the one who has your guns, though, and I haven't done anything with them. I was trying to explain to the major here when you came busting in."

"I did not 'bust in.' I came through the door, and I have as much right as you to be here. Possibly more."

"I don't doubt that, either," Fargo said. "Why don't you relax and let me finish explaining things?"

"Why do you not tell me who you are, first?"

"I'm afraid my manners are lacking," Wellman said. He was a short, trim man, everything about him looking neat and in place, from the hair on his head to his small mustache. "Señorita Cruz, the gentleman you're speaking to is Skye Fargo, called the Trailsman by some, and this other gentleman is Mr. Alvie Vernon, a deputy marshal from San Antonio."

Adelita gave a soft scornful snort at hearing Fargo described as a gentleman, but she said nothing.

"If you should be angry at anyone, I would be that person," Wellman continued. "I'm the army's representative here, and it's the army that's lost your guns. Tell her, Fargo."

Fargo had been going over with Wellman what had happened when Adelita had come storming into the office, having heard some scrap of gossip about the guns. Fargo started again and told the story as best he could.

"The soldiers who lost the rifles are out searching now," Fargo said, "but I don't think they'll have any better luck than

I did. Alvie and I came here to see if we could get any ideas from Major Wellman or his men."

"Let's all sit down," Wellman said, "so we can talk about this more comfortably and quietly."

They all took seats, though Adelita looked to Fargo as if she might run outside any minute to start looking for Ike and the guns. She wasn't one to take things calmly.

"I still do not understand why you could not find this man Ike," Adelita said to Fargo.

Fargo explained again about the hard ground and the difficulty of finding tracks.

"And it was just plain ol' rock, sometimes," Alvie added. "No way to do any trackin', no matter how good you are."

"I might be able to help you with this, señorita," Wellman said. "I know where some of the traders hole up."

"We'd need to know which ones Ike was lookin' for," Alvie said.

"I'd expect him to go to the nearest," Wellman said. "If he knows where they are."

"He must know," Fargo said. "Otherwise, he wouldn't have taken the rifles."

"He might hold them for ransom, instead," Adelita said. "Much good that would do him."

Ike had probably considered that, Fargo thought. He might even try it if the Comancheros turned him down.

"I think we can assume he knows the whereabouts of some of the traders," Wellman said. "I think we can also assume that he would be looking for a group that had money and that didn't mind dealing with somebody of his caliber."

"Which is mighty damn low," Alvie said, "and pardon me for cussin', ma'am."

"I can cuss as well as you or any man should I want to," Adelita snapped.

Fargo grinned, but he made sure not to let her see him do it. She seemed to Fargo to take everything as a challenge. She'd probably had to prove herself time and again to get to her current position with the revolutionaries.

"At any rate," Wellman said, trying to ignore the exchange, "I believe that the trading band loosely governed by a man named Speight is the one our rifle thief would head for."

"Lorne Speight?" Alvie said, looking as if he'd like to spit on the floor.

"Indeed," Wellman said. "The very man."

"He's the worst of 'em, I've heard. Just as soon kill you as not."

"The worst and the richest," Wellman said. "You seem to know the reason why."

"I've heard the stories," Alvie said.

"What stories are those?" Adelita asked.

"They say he's not just a trader," Alvie told her. "He and his men dress up like the Comanches or Apaches and rob travelers on the El Paso road. The Indians get the blame and Speight and his gang get the swag."

"All that appears to be true," Wellman said, "but appearances aren't enough to put a man in prison. No one's ever been able to prove anything against Speight."

"We don't need to prove anything," Fargo said. "We just need to get those rifles back and take Ike to San Antonio for his trial."

"And his hangin'," Alvie said. "Where's this Speight holed up?"

"Not too far from here, as it happens."

"Another good reason why Ike'd be headin' for him," Alvie said. "Easy to get to. Tell us where, and me and Fargo will go after him."

"You'll need more than two men to take on Speight."

"I will go, too," Adelita said. "And my men with me."

"Even that might not be enough," Wellman said.

"We can hook up with the soldiers who were transporting the rifles," Fargo said. "That should give us plenty of men."

"Even so, Speight's well protected."

"You still ain't told us where," Alvie pointed out.

Wellman stood up and walked over to a map pinned to the wall behind Alvie's chair. Alvie stood to look, and Fargo and Adelita joined him.

"This is Camp Hudson," Wellman said, tapping the map with his forefinger. He tapped the map again. "And this is where Speight is purported to be. Follow the creek to Devil's River, and then head into Dead Man's Canyon."

The spot he indicated was about fifteen miles away, at least a day's travel, considering the country they'd be going through, Fargo thought.

"Does *purported* mean what I think it does?" Alvie said.

"If you think it means that he might not be there," Wellman said, "you're right. I think the information might be correct, however. This area is hard to get to, and it has a number of hills and caves. It's also a dead-end canyon. One way in and one way out. Excellent for ambushes. It's just the kind of place someone like Speight might choose."

Adelita wasn't deterred by the description of Speight's location. She stood up and said, "We leave now."

"Hold on," Fargo said, standing as well. "We'll need some supplies. We might not get back here as soon as you seem to think we will."

Adelita glared at him. "You get your supplies. My men and I will ride in an hour. If you choose to ride with us, fine. If not, that is fine, too."

"Traveling at night through that country can be dangerous," Wellman said.

"I am not afraid," Adelita told him. "I must have those rifles." She looked at Fargo. "Are you afraid? Or will you ride with us?"

"We'll ride with you," Fargo said.

"If we can find them soldiers, we'll be all right," Alvie said.

Adelita shook her head. "We do not need them."

Fargo wasn't so sure, but now wasn't the time to argue about it.

He figured he and Adelita would have plenty of arguments later on.

Fargo and Alvie went to the mess hall, where they managed to get a quick meal. After they ate, they filled their canteens and found that Wellman had requisitioned some supplies for them. They packed the supplies on their mounts and went back to his office to thank him.

"You're likely to have trouble with that woman," Wellman said. "She's not going to want to take orders from anybody. If you meet up with the troops, that won't sit well with the sergeant."

"Won't sit too well with Fargo, either, I bet," Alvie said. "How 'bout it, Fargo?"

"We'll get along," Fargo said. "We're both after the same thing."

"Maybe not," Alvie said. "She wants those guns. We want the guns, but we want Ike, too."

"We'll get him."

"Damn right," Alvie said.

They left Camp Hudson around three o'clock. Adelita was determined to travel through the night, but Fargo knew that wasn't going to be possible. They didn't know the country, and even with a full moon it would still be treacherous to try. And an ambush would be far too easy for someone like Ike to set up.

They made good time until twilight, when seeing things got trickier in the dusky light. They had to slow down, even though Adelita complained about it.

She'd already complained about a good many things, including the fact that Fargo was leading them. Alvie had explained to her that Fargo was the best tracker there was, and she had laughed.

"He found no tracks before. What makes you think he can find them now?"

"He can find the trail to where Speight's got his Comancheros hid if anybody can. You and your men might can follow a map, but Fargo can find his way without one now that he knows where the place is. You better settle down and let him do what he does better than anybody."

Adelita settled down, but having Fargo in the lead didn't make her happy. She became even less happy when night fell and Fargo said it was time to make camp. They'd been following the route of the creek, and Fargo led them to a gently sloping clearing near the creek bank.

Adelita and her men followed him, but Fargo knew that the men were just waiting for a word from her to go on toward Devil's River, leaving Fargo and Alvie to spend the night by the creek without them. If she'd told the men to kill him and Alvie, cut them open, fill their bodies with rocks, and sink them in the creek, they'd have been happy to do that, too.

"You are very sure of yourself," Adelita said, dismounting near Fargo and the Ovaro. "You expect us to follow your orders, but we are not subject to you. We do what we want to do, not what you order us to do."

Fargo pulled the saddle off the Ovaro and put it on the

ground. The moon was rising, showing an edge above the trees. The trickle of the creek made a soft noise nearby.

"Here's how it is," Fargo said, as he began to wipe down the Ovaro with a blanket. "I think it's best that we stop for the night and travel again at sunrise. You say you don't have to follow my lead, and that's true. If you want to go blundering around in the dark, then go right on ahead. Don't expect me and Alvie to help out if anything happens to you, though. You'll be responsible."

Adelita tensed and fingered the whip at her waist. "Men do not often talk to me in such a tone."

Fargo shrugged. "Maybe not."

Adelita studied him for a moment. Gradually the tension went out of her, and she ordered her men to make camp.

Fargo continued to rub down the Ovaro. When he was done, he gave the big stallion some grain and led it down to the creek to drink.

Alvie joined him at the creek with his pinto.

"You and Miz Cruz seem to be hittin' it off," Alvie said drily. "I think she likes you."

"About like that rattlesnake did yesterday," Fargo said, "and you saw how that turned out."

"Turned out fine for you. Not so much for the snake. You wouldn't think Adelita was a snake, would you?"

Fargo grinned. "Not even close. You want to take the first watch?"

"Look here," Alvie said. "Why don't you ask her about settin' a watch? Let her think you're givin' in a little."

Fargo started to say he wasn't about to give in, but he thought better of it.

"You're a smart man, Alvie," he said.

Alvie laughed. "That might be the first time anybody's ever called me that."

Fargo clapped him on the back and walked over to where Adelita was talking to the men. He stopped and asked if he could speak to her.

Her eyes flashed at him. "You have more orders for me?"

"Nothing like that," he said.

"Very well."

She said something to the men in Spanish, and she and Fargo walked a few yards away.

"Speak," she said.

"I wanted to ask you about setting a guard for the night," Fargo said. "Do you want me and Alvie to do it, or would you prefer having your own men take the watch?"

Adelita studied Fargo's face. She was so tall that her eyes were almost on a level with his, and even in the gathering dark he could feel them boring into him.

"You are a strange man," she said. "Different from others I have known."

"I'm just making an offer."

"Yes, but you did not have to. You could have ordered me to see if I obeyed."

"I don't like to give orders. I'm just trying to do what's best for all of us."

"Of course." She continued to study him. "I believe I will ask my men to stand the watch. It will be for the best."

"Fine," Fargo said. "Alvie and I could use a good night's sleep."

Adelita turned and went back to her men, who were squatting on their haunches or standing silently as they waited for her to return. She gave them their orders in Spanish, and Fargo went to see Alvie, who was building a fire.

"Gonna have me some coffee and beans," Alvie said. "You want some?"

"Sounds fine," Fargo said. "I haven't had any army beans

for a while. Adelita will be setting the guard. You and I can get some rest."

"Best news I've heard today. Maybe I'm a smart fella, after all."

"Just make the coffee," Fargo said.

"Yes, sir, Mr. Fargo. I'll do that right now."

"You worried that I'm giving you too many orders?" Fargo asked.

Alvie laughed. "Go ahead and give 'em. Makin' coffee beats pushin' a broom at the jail."

It was around midnight when Fargo heard the noise. It wasn't much of a sound, no more than a leaf brushing a shoulder, but it was more than enough to bring Fargo awake.

He'd put his bedroll down in the trees away from the creek bank. The sandy bank would have been a little more comfortable, but Fargo didn't like being out in the open when he slept. He preferred to be hidden away a little bit. He figured that if anybody tried to slip up on the sleeping men and managed to get past the guard, he'd be clear of the trouble and able to help out.

Unless somebody stumbled across him on the way to the creek and made sure he wasn't able to help.

Fargo didn't open his eyes, but his fingers closed on the butt of his pistol, which was never far from his side even when he was sleeping.

"You do not have to pretend that you are asleep, Señor Fargo," Adelita said. "I did not come here to kill you."

Fargo released his grip on the pistol and sat up. "Why did you come here, then?"

"I wanted to find out."

"Find out what?"

"If you are as much of a man as you think you are."

"How did you plan to do that?"

"Like this," Adelita said.

She unbuttoned her shirt and pulled it off.

"That's a good start," Fargo said. He wasn't wearing his buckskins under his blanket. "You have any other ideas?"

Adelita knelt beside him and pulled back the blanket that covered him. She looked him over in the faint moonlight that filtered through the trees.

"Standing at attention already," she said with what sounded to Fargo like a bit of admiration, "and so very straight and tall."

Fargo wondered exactly what Adelita was trying to prove, and whether she was trying to prove it to herself or to him. Whatever the situation was, Fargo knew he wasn't going to resist what was about to happen. He could work out the ramifications of it later, if he still wanted to.

Adelita removed the rest of her clothing and lay beside him on the blanket he'd spread on the ground. She took a firm hold of his erect shaft with one hand and began to slide her fingers slowly up and down, letting them linger on the sensitive tip.

Fargo let his own fingers wander over Adelita's lush breasts. Her nipples jutted out, hard as stone, and he took one in his mouth, savoring it for a moment.

Adelita's breath caught, but she continued to massage his member as Fargo's hand moved lower, caressing her flat stomach before it encountered the thicket of hair at the base. His hand lingered there for a moment before his finger slipped into the slippery cleft between her legs.

This time the catch in Adelita's breath was louder. Fargo's finger had found the sensitive little bud that it was searching for. He massaged it slowly, and Adelita pressed her pelvis against his palm with increasing urgency. Her breath came faster, and her hand fairly flew on his shaft.

Fargo kissed her, and she returned the kiss with passion. Their tongues tangled for a moment before they broke apart, and Adelita threw her leg over Fargo to mount him.

He let her, and she settled herself on him, sinking on him until he was sheathed fully inside her. She leaned forward until the tips of her breasts burned against his chest and then gyrated her hips.

After a bit of that, she raised herself, slid back down, raised herself again. Faster and faster she rode him, gasping with pleasure as Fargo thrust into her.

Fargo was nearing the point of explosion, but he wasn't quite ready for things to end. He put his hands on Adelita's hips, grasped her firmly and rolled over on top of her.

Her body stiffened and she resisted briefly, but she soon relaxed and gave in. Fargo plunged into her, relishing the heat of her and feeling her womanhood grip him tightly as if to hold him there, though that was impossible. Soon he was moving rapidly, and Adelita was moving as well, joining him in the final frenzy that led to their release.

Fargo contained himself as Adelita squirmed under him in the grip of passion the likes of which Fargo had seldom seen. Her head was back, her mouth open, her eyes tightly shut.

She inhaled deeply and wrapped her arms around Fargo, pulling herself to him. Her mouth was at his ear.

"Now," she said. "Now!"

Fargo wasn't sure whether it was a demand or a request, but by that point he was past caring. He held back no longer but emptied himself into her with burst after burst as she clung to him and exhaled one prolonged *Ah!* into his ear.

Afterward, they lay side by side on the blanket. The big moon was going down but still visible through the trees.

"Your belief in yourself is not misplaced," Adelita said.

"I didn't give you any orders."

"No, nor did I order you. We did what two people do, and it was good."

"It was better than that," Fargo said.

"Yes. It was. But it can be even better than that."

"Are we going to prove that?"

"We are," Adelita said," "if you are up to it." She reached for him. "And I see that you are."

"Yes," Fargo said, "I believe I am."

8

They broke camp early the next morning, not long after sunrise. Fargo and Adelita hadn't had much sleep, but they didn't let on before the others that anything had changed. Fargo figured they had their suspicions, especially Alvie, but nobody said anything.

Not that anything had really changed. He and Adelita had accepted each other as equals, but he'd been willing to do that from the start. Adelita was the one who'd been bothered, but now she knew Fargo in the most intimate way possible and no longer considered him a threat to her authority. She hadn't taken control of him as she might have hoped to, but neither had he tried to command her. They'd shared the experience, and that was as it should be.

"What about them soldiers?" Alvie said as they broke camp. "You reckon we'll run into 'em today?"

"That depends on whether they could follow Ike's trail better than I could," Fargo said, "or whether they know where Lorne Speight's hiding out. Or whether they get lucky and stumble across something."

"We could use those boys. Speight's not gonna be easy to get to."

"If Ike can get to him, we can get to him."

"Ike has somethin' they want. We don't."

"But we're smarter. Or you are. Remember?"

"I might be smart about women," Alvie said, "but that's 'cause of all my experience with 'em. Comancheros is a whole 'nother story."

He had that right, Fargo thought.

Ike arrived at the entrance to Dead Man's Canyon about noon. He didn't like the looks of the place at all. The entrance was flanked by high rocks, not mountains, but high enough to be impressive considering the mostly open country around them.

He couldn't see much past the entrance from where he sat on one of the mules that he'd been riding to give his horse a rest. He knew that the canyon wound down among high rock walls until it branched off into two smaller, much shorter, canyons. All three of them ended at blank rock walls. That was what his cousins had told him, at least.

"Speight's in the one on the right," one of them had said, "but it's not likely that anybody'd get that far without being shot. He has men all along the main canyon, and they all have guns. He's not a man who likes company."

Ike worried a little about that, but he didn't look like anybody who'd be a threat to Speight. He was just a man with a couple of mules to trade, as far as anybody could see. If they'd let him in, he could tell them what else he had, and since it was well hidden, he didn't think they'd kill him.

He wasn't certain about that last part, though. They might think he was just a liar and do away with him. Or they could wait until he led them to the guns and kill him after they had them.

That was too far in the future to worry about, however, so Ike clucked at the mule and rode on down to the canyon entrance.

Nobody shot him when he got there, so he rode on, passing into the shade of the canyon walls. He had the feeling he was being watched, but although he scanned the rocks on both sides of him, he couldn't spot anyone. Once he thought he may have caught the glint of a rifle barrel, but he couldn't be sure that's what it was. Might've been just his eyes playing tricks on him.

He went through the canyon like that, passing from sun to shade, watching the rocks, and seeing nothing other than an occasional bird and one jackrabbit that ran into the brush along the trail.

The canyon was about a mile long, Ike figured. He came to the place where it continued for a little way ahead and the two other canyons forked off in other directions. He turned the mule's head and headed into the one on the right.

The man appeared in front of him as if by magic. First he wasn't there and then he was. Ike blinked his eyes twice to be sure the man wasn't a mirage.

He wasn't. He was real, big and bearded, and he was holding a rifle that was pointed right at Ike.

"You'd better have a good reason for being here," the man said. "Else I'll shoot you where you sit."

"I have a good reason," Ike said, proud that his voice was steady. "I have something to trade."

The man looked him over. "Not very damn much. Two sorry-assed mules and a horse."

"I got better than this."

Another man stepped out from behind a rock. He might have been the first man's twin. He had a rifle, too.

"What about it, Hank?" the first man said. "Kill him and take his livestock?"

"Might as well kill the livestock, too, Rufe, sorry as it is. Wouldn't do us any good."

Ike knew he didn't mean that. The mules were stout and plenty healthy.

"You might be sorry if you do," Ike said, his voice not as steady as it had been. "I told you, I got other stuff. Speight would like to hear about it."

"I guess you want us to take you to him," Rufe said.

"That's the idea," Ike told him.

Rufe and Hank looked at each other. Hank shrugged and said, "You take him in."

"Hell, why do I have to do it? Speight'll have my guts for garters if this fella's not worth the trouble."

"It's your turn. I took in the last one."

"Yeah," Rufe said. "He was a tough one. Took him a long time to die."

Ike's mouth was dry. He swallowed hard, hoping the two men didn't notice.

"You follow me," Rufe told Ike.

He went back behind the rock and came out riding a horse that Ike didn't think looked one bit better than his own. He didn't think it would be smart to point that out to Rufe, however, so he didn't. He did what Rufe said and followed him.

Fargo's bunch rode most of the day without catching sight of the soldiers who'd been escorting the wagonload of guns. Fargo thought they could be miles away, or they could be close. It was impossible to say.

He'd had better luck with Ike. He'd picked up the trail of the two mules and the horse a while back.

"Gotta be Ike," Alvie said. "No wagon, though."

"He cached it somewhere," Fargo said. "Probably hid it. Thinks Speight can't find it."

"If this Speight is the kind of man you say he is," Adelita said, "he will have a way to find it."

Fargo knew she meant torture. He wondered if Ike had thought of that.

"Well, he's ahead of us, whatever happens to him," Alvie said. "That's fine with me. I wouldn't want to be in his boots about now."

They were sitting on their horses about two miles from the canyon. Adelita was beside them, with her men a little way behind. They could see the canyon rocks rising up from the flat landscape.

"He does not have the rifles," Adelita said. "We could find them."

"What do you think, Alvie," Fargo said. "Could you follow his back trail?"

"Sure, till it hit the rock. After that, it'd be just luck if I found the wagon."

"And the same for me," Fargo said. "We need Ike, and we need him alive."

"How will we get him?" Adelita asked.

"I know how we won't," Alvie said. "I'd as soon ride into a wildcat den as into that canyon. At least I could see the wildcats, and they wouldn't have guns."

"Even if we do get in," Adelita said, "we do not know which branch of the canyon this Speight is in."

"Not the main one," Fargo said. "He wouldn't like it there. So he's on the right or the left."

"Still a bad deal," Alvie said. "We'd never get to either one of 'em."

"One of us might," Fargo said.

"Which one?" Adelita said.

Fargo grinned. "Me."

Adelita bristled. "Why not me? Why not one of my men?"

"Because I'm better than your men."

"Better than me?"

"I didn't say that. Maybe I'm not. What I do know for sure is that we can't all go."

"You think you can get Ike out of there by yourself?"

"I can try."

"Ike stole them rifles all by hisself," Alvie said. "If he could do that, Fargo could probably take on the whole state of Texas."

Adelita didn't look reassured. "If you do go alone, what about the rest of us?"

"If I get Ike, they'll come boiling out of that canyon like hornets some kid stirred with a stick," Fargo told her. "You'll have to deal with them."

"And if they don't?"

"Then you can come in after me."

"There's just eleven of us," Alvie said. "There's bound to be as many as fifty of them. I don't much like them odds."

"Are you afraid?" Adelita asked. "Because my men and I are not."

"I'm not afraid," Alvie said. "Just careful. I didn't get to be this old by going up against five men at one time."

"Some of that number will be women and children," Fargo said. "You won't have to worry about them. Probably not more than thirty men. Could be only twenty."

"That sounds a little better," Alvie said, "but look here. We don't know for sure Speight won't just buy those rifles and let Ike go on his way."

"You really believe that?"

"It could happen like that," Alvie insisted. He looked off into the distance. "Ain't very damn likely, though, is it?"

"Not very," Fargo said. "If it does happen like that, you'll be here to stop them from getting the guns when they go after them."

Alvie rubbed the back of his neck. "You reckon they know we're out here?"

Fargo hadn't seen the reflection of the sun on binoculars or rifle barrels, but that didn't mean he hadn't missed it.

"They do not know," Adelita said. "I would feel it if they knew."

Fargo didn't question her. He'd had feelings like that before, so she might even be right.

"Well, now that we've talked it out," Alvie said, "who's got a plan?"

"I'm going in," Fargo said. He looked at Adelita. "I'll leave the rest to you."

Adelita looked around the countryside, taking it in with calculating eyes. After a few seconds, she turned to Fargo and said, "We will be ready."

Fargo didn't ask what they'd be ready for. He simply nodded and rode away. His idea was that Speight would be in the right-hand branch of the canyon. Most people were right-handed and tended to turn that way when given a choice. Besides, using the left hand was associated with bad luck by a lot of people. Not for any logical reason, but some people didn't care much about logic. Fargo also remembered that on Wellman's map the right-hand branch had been somewhat longer and more crooked. That feature would appeal to someone looking for concealment.

Fargo also figured that Speight would be at the very end of the canyon, backed up against the wall so that nobody could get at him from behind.

That was a lot of assumptions, and if Fargo was wrong, Ike might be dead by the time he got there, if he wasn't dead already. Fargo didn't put much stock in the idea that Ike would be able to talk Speight into paying him for the rifles. Speight wasn't that kind of man.

Alvie Vernon wasn't the only one who'd heard of Speight.

Fargo knew about him, too, and there were those who said that he was more vicious when torturing his enemies than any Comanche. The Comanche admired bravery and to some of their warriors, to torture a man was to put him to the ultimate test. As Fargo knew, it was a test that no one passed.

Speight didn't care about testing a man's courage. To him, torture was two things. It was a way to get information, but it was also something that Speight enjoyed. Or so the story was told. Fargo couldn't vouch for it. If it was even half true, however, Ike would never ride out of the canyon, not unless Fargo could bring him out.

As Fargo rode, he wondered why he was bothering with Ike. The man was a killer, and if he got back to San Antonio, he would face a hanging rope. But the rope was justice, Fargo thought. Torture was something else—brutality, mainly—and it had nothing at all to do with justice. If Fargo could get Ike away from Speight, he would. It was only right to let the law have the last word on him.

And then there were the rifles. Adelita wanted them. The government wanted her to have them, and only Ike knew where they were. Fargo didn't think the soldiers who had lost them would be able to find them. He had to get Ike to lead the way to them.

Just how he was going to do that wasn't clear to him. If he was right about where Speight was located, then Speight would be likely to guard his back. But maybe not as carefully as his front. After all, there was no way a large force could get into his camp from the rear, not without giving him plenty of warning. There'd be a guard up in the rocks somewhere, but Fargo guessed there would be no more than two, and maybe only one. Getting past one man wouldn't pose much of a problem.

The problem would be finding Ike, freeing him, and getting him out without both of them getting killed.

Fargo knew it wasn't going to be easy.

Ike was buck-naked, spread-eagle on the hard-packed earth in Speight's encampment. His arms and legs were stretched tight and tied to stakes pounded into the ground. The sun burned down from the clear blue sky, forcing him to keep his eyes closed most of the time.

He didn't know how things had gone so wrong, but they had. And for once he didn't have a plan.

It wasn't his fault, damn it. How was he to know that Speight wouldn't even listen to him? The man was crazy—that was all there was to it.

Ike had done everything right. He'd followed Rufe into the camp, where the women and children had made fun of him and even thrown things at him. He didn't mind that. Let 'em have their fun. The payoff was getting closer all the time.

Except that it wasn't. Ike had been dead wrong about that, and soon he was likely to be just plain dead.

The camp was mostly tents, with a few small wooden buildings, just dry tinder that looked like a good wind would blow them down, if there was ever a wind in the canyon. Speight was in one of them, and that was where Rufe took Ike.

The interior of the building smelled like something had died in it, but Ike thought it was just that Speight didn't bathe very often, if ever. There was a rickety table on one side of the room with food scraps lying on it. The scraps had been there a while and didn't help make the smell any better.

Speight himself was an unimposing little man who regarded him from where he sat in a straight-backed chair tilted back against the wall near the only window in the single room. It was hard to judge, but Ike guessed he couldn't have been more than five feet tall. It was hard to say much about his face because it was virtually covered with a thick black beard, from which his wild eyes peered out.

As soon as he saw those eyes, Ike knew he was in trouble, big trouble. They seemed to be glowing in the dim light in the room. They were the eyes of a madman.

"This fella wanted to see you," Rufe said, pushing Ike through the door.

Speight grunted. There was something in his hands. It looked like a book. Ike couldn't believe the man was reading a book.

"What's he want?" Speight said.

His voice was flat and toneless. Ike thought that if a dead man could talk, he'd sound just like Speight.

"Says he has something to trade," Rufe told him. "All's I saw was two mules and a horse. Might do for eatin'. Not much else."

"Kill him," Speight said, and turned his eyes back to his reading.

"What?" Ike said. He couldn't have heard what he thought he heard. "What?"

Speight looked up, his eyes shining in the forest of his beard. He raised the book he was holding in one hand and gestured with it in Ike's direction.

"'Any outsider who comes near shall be put to death.' Numbers three:ten." He lowered the book. "Kill him."

"Wait," Ike said, trying not to sound as desperate as he was. "Wait. You can't kill me. I have more than a horse and mules. I have Henry rifles."

Speight studied him for a long time, his eyes burning into him. "Where?"

That was more like it, Ike thought. He still had a chance if he just played things right.

"They're hidden. But I know the way to where they are. I can show you. I'll sell 'em to you for a good price. You'll see."

"Where are they?"

Ike knew it would be a big mistake to answer that question. He'd be dead as soon as the words were out of his mouth.

"I can take you," he said.

"Save us the time and trouble," Speight said in that dead man's voice of his. "Tell me where they are."

"I can't tell you. I have to show you."

"Tell me now, or tell me later," Speight said. "It makes no difference to me."

"I'll take you to them, and you can pay me."

Speight seemed to lose interest in him. The fire in his eyes died. He said to Rufe, "You know what to do."

"Sure," Rufe said, and he hit Ike in the back of his head with his rifle, knocking him down and out.

That was all Ike knew for a while, and now here he was, blistering in the sun, with a bunch of women heating something in a fire close by. Ike had a feeling he wouldn't like what they were going to do to him. He might as well tell them what they wanted to know before they started burning him and cutting him.

But if he told them, they'd kill him. Maybe they were going to kill him, anyway, but he'd hold out as long as he could.

He didn't think that would be very long.

Fargo came to the scattering of rocks in back of the canyon without any trouble, and he didn't think he'd been spotted. He tied the Ovaro to a bush well away from the canyon rim. The big horse looked down at the ground and started to crop the sparse prairie grass.

Fargo left him there and began to make his way through

the rocks. The going was fairly easy. There was a gentle slope up to the rim, but there were plenty of rocks and bushes to provide cover.

As he moved along, Fargo kept a watch for the guard that he knew had to be there, somewhere or other. He didn't think the man would be too alert, because it was almost a certainty that no one else had ever tried to come at Speight from behind.

Fargo knew he could be wrong. Speight might not be in this branch of the canyon at all.

But Fargo wasn't wrong. He spotted the guard, who was leaned back against a boulder, taking advantage of the little shade it gave him, his hat pulled down over his eyes. He was either asleep or near to it.

Fargo hated to kill a man for no reason at all, especially a man who had no way of defending himself. As he slipped closer, he pulled his big Colt.

When he reached the boulder, the man stirred and pushed up his hat. His eyes widened when he saw Fargo, and he reached for the rifle that lay across his lap.

Before he reached it, Fargo had clubbed him with the barrel of the Colt, and he slumped sideways against the boulder.

Fargo couldn't take a chance that the guard would wake up and give the alarm, so he gagged the man with a piece of his shirt and tied his hands and feet with strips of cloth cut from his pants. The man might work free, but not anytime soon.

Leaving the man where he lay, Fargo took the rifle and climbed down through the rocks at the rim of the canyon. He looked down and saw the tents and buildings of the camp. A little corral held some horses and mules. Like the rest of the camp, it was flimsily constructed.

In the middle of things was Ike, and he was in a hell of a mess.

Fargo knew what Ike was in for now that he was staked

out. First they'd burn his feet and hands, then maybe cut them off. After that, they'd start on the more tender parts. Then they'd skin him. Give Ike credit, though, he must not have told them where the rifles were. That was the only reason he was still alive.

If Fargo wanted the rifles, he had to get Ike out of there, and quickly.

A fragment of a poem Fargo had heard years before popped into his head. He didn't remember where he'd heard it, but it had likely been declaimed by some half-drunk medicine show performer. The poem was about some battle or other. Fargo didn't remember much about the poem and nothing at all about the battle. He just remembered a couple of lines of verse:

The Assyrian came down like the wolf on the fold,
And his cohorts were gleaming in purple and gold. . . .

Fargo was wearing buckskins, he didn't have any cohorts, and he wasn't sure what an Assyrian was. But if he was going to save Ike, he was going to have to come down on the little camp below him like a wolf on a sheepfold.

Fargo estimated that the canyon was about a quarter of a mile deep, more or less. The sides weren't steep. A man could get down them without breaking his neck if he was careful, but the Trailsman didn't have time to be careful.

He went back to the man he'd knocked out. The man was awake, but he wasn't able to do anything other than squirm around while Fargo cut the rest of this clothing to ribbons.

With the strips of cloth, Fargo tied bundles of dried brush together, with a rock in the middle of the brush. He made five bundles. That would have to do. He gathered his bundles and went back up to the top of the rim.

He checked the larger rocks around him and found a few

he thought would do to start a small avalanche. A big avalanche would be even better, but he had to make do with what was available.

Glancing down into the canyon, Fargo saw that the women were about to begin work on Ike. They stood over him, holding the heated iron, putting it close to his face, so he could feel the fiery metal and know what was in store for him.

Fargo didn't let himself hurry. If Ike got burned, that was too bad for Ike. But if Fargo made a mistake, it would be the end of him and Ike both. He took a lucifer from his pocket.

He was about to strike it and light the first bundle when he heard Ike scream.

Ike knew what they were going to do. He'd known all along, but at that instant it became real, and he knew he couldn't take it. He'd thought he could stand the pain to prolong his life, but it wasn't going to be like that.

Ike's stomach churned, and when the red-hot iron almost touched the skin of his face, his fear got the best of him. He screamed and wet himself. The women jumped back, pointing at him and laughing.

"I'll tell, I'll tell!" Ike screamed. "Where's Speight? I'll tell!"

The women looked at him, and he could see the disappointment on their faces. They thought he was a coward, but what the hell? He wasn't going to let them burn him. Anything was better than that, at least for the moment. He'd tell Speight where the rifles were, and Speight could kill him. He could stand that better than to be burned all over his body.

Tears came to Ike's eyes. He didn't want to die, but he couldn't stand the unendurable pain he knew was coming.

Speight came out of his building and walked over to Ike, his shadow falling across him. Ike heard his dead man's voice.

"'A coward dies a thousand times before his death.'"

A little of Ike's courage returned, enough to let him say, "To hell with you, you bastard. Cut me loose. I'll tell you where the rifles are."

"Tell me now."

Ike had no intention of telling him. As scared as he was, his mind was still working. Now he had a plan.

"I can't tell you. I know where the place is, but I can't tell you how to get there. I'll take you. You can have the guns. Just let me go after you get them. That's all I care about."

Anything to stay alive a little longer. That was all Ike cared about.

Speight didn't go along with it. "You'll tell me. It won't take long. Let me call the women."

Ike struggled to keep himself from screaming. "Goddamn it, I said I can't tell you. You can burn me, but I still can't tell you. You have to let me take you there!"

Speight smiled. It was a terrible thing to see. "I don't need the rifles that bad. I'd rather stay here and watch the women work on you than to have them."

Ike knew that Speight meant it. Though the heat of the sun on Ike's skin was almost as intense as the heat from the iron, he was suddenly as cold as if he'd plunged into a mountain stream at snowmelt time.

Speight pulled a pair of dirty leather gloves out of his back pocket. He looked down at Ike as he pulled first one and then the other on his hands. He clasped his hands together to smooth out the leather. When he was satisfied with the way they felt, he went over to the fire and pulled out one of the heated rods.

"Come to think of it," Speight said, walking back over to where Ike lay, "I'd kind of like to work on you, myself."

* * *

127

Fargo was surprised to see the man come out of the building. It had to be Speight, considering the way the women deferred to him. Fargo couldn't hear what he was saying to Ike, but he figured Ike must have decided that he didn't want to be tortured. Fargo couldn't really blame him.

The rifle Fargo had taken from the guard was an 1853 Sharps. It hadn't been well cared for, but Fargo figured it would still shoot. He didn't think he could hit Speight with it at such a great distance and shooting downhill besides, but he might scare him.

Fargo sighted the man in and pulled the trigger.

Speight spun around. Fargo didn't know if he'd been hit or not, and he didn't have time to look. He dropped the rifle, struck the lucifer, and set fire to the bundles of brush and threw them one after the other. He hoped at least one of them would land on a tent or a building, but he didn't have time to look at the results. He was too busy pushing rocks over the edge of the canyon rim.

As soon as he got the rocks rolling, Fargo began running behind them, a reckless run down the steep slope that he hoped wouldn't end with him lying dead at the bottom.

He fell once and rolled over twice, but he regained his feet and continued his headlong progress.

One of the buildings was burning. So was one of the tents. People were milling around, yelling and trying to figure out what was happening. Some of them ran to the building that was on fire. Brush behind another of the buildings was burning. The horses ran around in the corral. One of the bigger rocks crashed into a house. Another one hit something, bounced, and slammed into a man before rolling over him.

Fargo hit the canyon floor bruised and scraped, but he kept right on running. Nobody was paying any attention to him. They might not even have known he was there. He pulled out his Colt, just in case.

Speight was nowhere to be seen, so if Fargo had hit him, he hadn't been killed. Fargo didn't have time to look for him. He had to get to Ike.

When Ike saw Fargo, his eyes bugged out so far that the Trailsman could have raked them off his face with a stick.

Fargo reached into his boot for the Arkansas toothpick and cut the rawhide thongs that held Ike to the stakes.

Ike jumped up. "Shit fire! What're you doing here?"

"Saving your sorry ass," Fargo said. "Come on."

Fargo ran for the corral, not looking to see if Ike was behind him. A man stepped in front of Fargo. Fargo shot him in the middle of the chest. The man toppled over, and Fargo ran on past.

The horses had calmed a bit when Fargo reached them. Fargo stuck the pistol in its holster and opened the corral gate. The horses swirled around and then ran through it.

As one of the horses passed him, the Trailsman seized its mane and pulled himself up onto its back. Leaning low over its neck, Fargo guided it toward Ike, who stared at him in shock.

Fargo swerved just in time. He reached down and grabbed Ike's forearm. The horse's forward motion and Fargo's grip pulled Ike along. Ike got the idea and allowed Fargo to draw him up behind him onto the horse's back. Ike wrapped his arms around Fargo and held on tight.

Fargo heard gunshots and bullets zip over him, but he wasn't hit. Neither was Ike. Fargo dug his heels into the horse's side, urging it to go faster.

A huge man ran out from behind a rock and put up his pistol. Before he could pull the trigger, the horse had reached him. Fargo kicked the man in the face and he fell backward.

The horse wasn't used to carrying a double load, but Fargo thought it would be a while before Speight's men rounded up the other spooked horses. Fargo and Ike should be able to get out of the canyon ahead of them. But they'd be coming.

Fargo knew he could count on that.

When they reached the canyon mouth, they surged up a slope and out into the open. Fargo saw no sign of Alvie, Adelita, or her men, but he knew they were out there somewhere. He hoped they wouldn't shoot him. Or Ike. He'd gone to a lot of trouble to save Ike.

As they rode through the brush, men rose up around them. They'd been completely hidden, even from Fargo's keen eyes. They were better than Fargo had thought they'd be. He pulled back on the horse's mane and managed to bring it to a halt.

"Damnation!" Alvie said. "I never thought I'd see the two of you ridin' together. Much less with one of you naked as a jaybird."

"Get off the horse, Ike," Fargo said, sliding off himself. "Maybe they can find you something to put on."

The men looked at Ike with amusement. Adelita didn't find anything funny about the situation.

"Is this the one who took the rifles?" she said.

"He's the one," Fargo said. He started to reload his pistol. "Get him some pants. Speight and his men won't be too far behind us."

Someone threw Ike a shirt. Someone else tossed him a belt and a pair of pants. Ike fumbled into them as quickly as he could.

"What about boots?" he asked.

"You do without them," Fargo told him. "Let's get ourselves under cover."

130

Adelita's men disappeared into bushes and grass that didn't appear big enough to hide them. So did she.

"Where are the horses?" Fargo asked Alvie.

Alvie pointed to his left. "Hid in them rocks."

Fargo slapped the rump of the horse he and Ike had ridden. It jumped and ran away.

Fargo pulled Ike down into some brush, and Alvie hid himself, too.

"What about a gun for me?" Ike said.

Fargo laughed. "You've got the nerve of a government mule. You just stay still and try not to get yourself killed."

Ike looked as if he might want to argue, but he didn't. He shut his mouth and lay down on the ground.

They didn't have long to wait. Speight and his gang rode out of the canyon, kicking up a cloud of dust behind them. They seemed to be following the tracks of the horse Fargo and Ike had ridden.

Adelita and her men waited until the riders were in their midst. Then they rose up and started shooting. Fargo and Alvie followed suit. Pistol and rifle fire drummed out a deadly tattoo.

Speight's bunch had Adelita's men outnumbered, but they were taken completely by surprise. Five of them were down almost at once, dead or wounded before they knew what was happening.

Fargo shot until his Colt was empty. As he reloaded, he watched Adelita. Her rifle jammed, and she threw it to the ground. She took the whip from its place at her belt and gave her wrist a backward flip. The whip uncoiled and she immediately slashed it forward.

It coiled around the neck of a rider. His hands went to his throat as if a snake encircled it. His face reddened, and he was jerked to the ground, his hands still trying to pry the braided leather from his throat. Adelita let him try.

"Cuidado!" one of her men cried.

Adelita dropped the whip and spun around, pulling the pistol from the holster on her left side. She fired it in almost the same motion, and Fargo fired as well. A man dropped off his horse only a few yards away from Adelita. She looked at Fargo.

"We both hit him," Fargo said.

"I hit him first."

Fargo grinned.

One of the riders, Speight no doubt, yelled something and turned back to the canyon. The few men who were left on their mounts jerked the horses' heads around and headed after him, back the way they'd come.

The air was full of dust and gun smoke. Fargo's ears rang from all the shooting. He started to say something, but he never got a chance.

Ike jumped up and hit him in the side of the head with a balled fist. As the Trailsman fell, Ike snatched the Colt from his hand. He didn't shoot Fargo. Instead he fired at the retreating riders. Fargo stood up in time to see one of them throw up his hands and fall off his horse.

Speight, Fargo thought. When it came to back-shooting, Ike turned out to be a lot better this time than when he'd ambushed Fargo and Alvie.

Or maybe this time he was just lucky.

9

They went to take a look at the man Ike had shot as soon as Fargo had taken back his pistol. It wasn't Speight, after all. Fargo should have known better. Ike had been trying to hit Speight, but he'd hit someone else instead. They looked at all the bodies, and Speight wasn't among them.

"Shit," Ike said. "I thought sure I'd got the son of a bitch."

"This one's a lot bigger than Speight," Fargo said. "Maybe that's why you hit him."

"I wanted to kill him. He was going to let those women burn me. Hell, he was going to burn me himself."

"He won't be burning anybody for a long time," Fargo said. "He doesn't have enough men left to back him up."

"Some of 'em are still alive," Alvie said.

Fargo looked back at the spot where the fighting had taken place. A couple of the men who'd attacked the group were still alive, all right, including the one with Adelita's whip still wrapped around his neck. She took it off just as he was about to choke to death.

"His face is as red as a possum's ass in pokeberry time," Alvie said as Adelita returned the whip to its place at her waist.

"He's not dead, though," Fargo said. "I don't think he cares about how his face looks right now."

"What'll we do with him? And those other two?"

"They aren't going anywhere," Fargo said.

One of Adelita's men was standing near them with his rifle ready. Both of them had shirts bloody from minor wounds.

Fargo left Alvie to watch Ike and walked over to where Adelita was talking to her men. One of them had his hat off because he was bleeding from a slight scalp wound. None of the others seemed to have a scratch.

Fargo asked Adelita what she'd like to do about the three Comancheros.

"Tell them to go back to their canyon," she said. "We have no use for them."

Fargo thought that was the best idea, and he'd have done the same. He told the man with the bruised throat what Adelita had said.

"You can come back out later and bury your dead," he added, though he didn't think Speight would care enough to do it. "We'll be gone in a little while."

"Sure," the man said.

Or something like that. Fargo couldn't make it out. The man's throat was damaged, and his voice sounded more like a wood rasp shaping a board than human speech.

The man still sat on the ground, and Fargo put down a hand to help him to his feet. The man looked at Fargo with suspicion at first, but after a second he put out his own hand.

"Take those others with you," Fargo told him as he pulled him up. "You can try to round up some horses, or you can walk. It's all the same to us."

This time the man didn't try to talk. He went to the two wounded men and gestured toward the canyon. They looked at the man guarding them, but he was no longer interested. The three Comancheros started to walk.

Adelita came over to Fargo and watched them until they

were fifty or sixty yards away. When they were well out of earshot, she turned to the Trailsman.

"We get the guns now?" she said.

"Depends on our friend Ike," Fargo said. "He's the one who knows where they are. He sure didn't want to tell Speight where they were."

"He will tell us." Adelita sounded sure of it.

"You planning to torture him if he doesn't?"

"I do not think we will have to."

"You could be right. Let's go ask him. Maybe he'll be so grateful to me for saving his worthless skin that he'll tell us without us even having to ask."

It didn't take them long to find out that Ike wasn't that grateful. He wasn't going to cooperate.

"I don't care if you did pull me out of that mess at Speight's camp," he told Fargo. "I can't help you with the rifles. I would if I could, but Speight's got 'em already. They're stashed in that canyon. You mighta got in there once, but you won't fool him again like that."

"He doesn't have enough men left to defend hisself," Alvie said. "We could get 'em easy."

"If they were there, we could," Fargo said. "Maybe. But they're not there."

Ike drew himself up as tall as he could. "Are you calling me a liar?"

His face was that of a little boy whose teacher had wrongly accused him of dipping a girl's pigtail into an inkwell.

"I guess I am," Fargo said. "But that's just because you are one. See, we followed your trail to the canyon, and the way I figure it, all Speight got out of the deal is a horse and two mules. A couple of the animals might've gotten away from him, by now, but there was never a wagon that went into the canyon with you."

"He picked the rifles up from me," Ike said. "Out there." He gestured vaguely toward the east. "Hid 'em somewhere. Didn't tell me where. I'd tell you if I knew, but I'm damned if I do."

"That's a good story," Fargo said, "but it's not the truth. You barely had time to get here from where you stole the rifles. You didn't tell Speight where they were, and even if you had, he couldn't have gotten them and hauled them back here by now. You tried to bargain with him, and he wouldn't listen. So you wound up staked to the ground. That's how it happened, and you might as well admit it."

Ike just looked at him.

"Tell us where the rifles are," Adelita said. "They are not yours. They belong to Benito Juárez."

"You don't look like any Benito to me," Ike said. "Who are you, anyway?"

"I am his representative in Texas, and you are a thief. You will tell us where the guns are."

"If I did know where they were, and if I told you, what would you give me? How about five hundred American dollars? Sound like a fair exchange to you?"

"How about if we just give you back to Speight," Alvie said. "He'll have you talkin' quick enough."

"You wouldn't do that," Ike said. He almost seemed to be enjoying himself. "If you did, you'd never get those rifles. Pay me. That's the easy way."

"If Juárez had the money, the government wouldn't be slippin' him the guns," Alvie said. "So it ain't as easy as you make it out to be."

"You're forgetting something, anyway," Fargo said.

"What's that?" Ike wanted to know.

"You killed a man in San Antonio. The marshal. He was a friend of mine."

"I'm sorry about the marshal. You say he's dead? I wouldn't accuse you of lying like you did me, but I don't know anything about that."

"Then you won't mind taking your chances in court after we get you back there."

Ike thought about that. "I have another idea. We can make that five hundred dollars and a couple of days' head start toward the border. Then you get the rifles."

"You would not find many friends in Mexico," Adelita told him.

Ike grinned. "I didn't say which border."

"It does not matter," Adelita said. Her hand went to her whip. "You will not be going anywhere."

"Now hold on just a minute," Ike said. "You're just as bad as Speight."

"I am not going to burn you," Adelita said. She held the whip handle in her right hand and let its braided leather length uncoil slowly as it passed through her left. "I am just going to teach you a lesson in truth telling."

Ike looked at Fargo. "You'd better stop her, Fargo. You don't want her to hurt me."

Fargo started to protest, but he kept his mouth shut. Let Adelita do as she would. He didn't think she'd hurt Ike any more than he deserved, and he deserved plenty.

"I don't think I give a damn if she hurts you," Fargo said. "Besides, she and I are equal partners in this. I abide by her decisions."

"Gracias," Adelita said. She flicked the whip out to its full length. "Now I will teach this little worm a lesson in crawling."

Ike wasn't inclined to be taught, and he didn't want to crawl. He turned to run, but two of Adelita's men grabbed him before he'd taken two steps. Fargo didn't think he'd have gone far with his feet bare, anyway.

The two men turned Ike around so that he faced Adelita. Fargo expected them to move away, but they must have trusted Adelita's skill. They stayed where they were, and one of them held Ike's right arm while the other held his left. They moved a step to each side, leaving a little room between themselves and Ike.

Ike seemed to relax, sagging between the men. They looked at him, and he snapped erect, jerking his arms in an attempt to break them free of the men's grip.

It didn't work. They hadn't let their guard down as Ike had hoped, and their hands didn't let go even for an instant.

"Damn it, Fargo!" Ike yelled. "Make 'em let go of my arms."

"All you have to do is tell them where the guns are," Fargo said.

"I can't tell anybody that. I don't know where they are."

Adelita snapped the whip and the tip cracked in the air like a shot.

"I swear I can't tell you," Ike said. "I can take you there, though. I know the way."

"If you can take us, you can tell us," Fargo said. "What do you think, Adelita?"

"I think you are right," she said.

The end of the whip snapped in front of Ike and a button flew off his borrowed shirt. Ike yelled, but he hadn't been touched.

The button flipped into the air, and when it started to fall, Fargo reached out and caught it.

Adelita smiled at him. "You are very quick."

"So they tell me," Fargo said.

"So am I," Adelita said.

The whip lashed out again and again until all the buttons were gone and the shirt hung open.

"Your name is Ike," Adelita said. "My English is good, and I will prove it by spelling your name on your chest."

"No, no, no," Ike said, "I'm telling you the truth. I can take you to the guns, and I will. You have to believe me."

The whip popped and the belt that held up Ike's pants parted at the buckle. The pants fell to his knees, exposing his genitals.

"Now there is something you do not often see," Adelita said. "A target so small that even I might miss it."

The men holding Ike's arms laughed. Ike didn't.

"You wouldn't," he said.

"I would," Adelita said. "Who will bet me five American dollars that I cannot take it off on the first try?"

"I'll cover that bet," Alvie said. "It's so damn little I can't even see it from here."

Ike put his knees together and turned to the side as best he could to protect himself.

"Please," he said. "I'll take you to the guns. I'd tell you where they were if I could. Let me take you. Please."

Adelita considered his words. "What do you think, Fargo?"

Fargo wasn't sure. Ike was a liar. That was an established fact, but would he lie under the threat of being unmanned by a bullwhip? He'd been ready to take Speight to the guns, but he hadn't told him where they were. Maybe he really couldn't put the location into words.

"I guess we could take a chance that he's telling the truth this time. He can't get away from us. We'll let him take us to the rifles."

"I hope you are right," Adelita said.

She gave one final glance at Ike and curled the whip. When she'd replaced it on her belt, she told her men to let Ike go.

"But tie him up. Hands and feet. And cover him. I do not like thinking of that tiny bird and its shriveled eggs."

The men laughed again. They let Ike pull up the pants and hold them on while they located a piece of rope to use as a belt. When he had the pants secure, they tied his hands.

"You can't tie my feet," Ike said. "I can't ride if you tie my damn feet."

"He's got a point there," Alvie said. "We could throw him across a saddle, though. Wouldn't bother me none if we did it thataway."

"Leave his feet free," Adelita said. "If he tries to escape, he will not get far before we catch him. And when we do, he will lose something he values."

Ike flinched as she stared at his crotch, and Alvie laughed.

"I believe he's prouder of that thing than he deserves to be," he said.

"Most men are," Adelita said. She smiled at Fargo. "Not all."

Alvie laughed again. "We better see if our horses're still where we left 'em. We can round up a couple of Speight's, too. Some of his folks won't be needin' 'em, and we need to get a ways from here before the buzzards get at 'em."

He pointed to the sky where the black birds were starting to circle high above. Fargo had seen them already. It was a shame not to bury a man you'd killed, to leave him for the buzzards, but they didn't have time to do any burying.

"Where'd you say those horses were?" he asked.

Alvie looked at Ike.

"I'll have to show you," he said.

They couldn't make it to the location of guns by nightfall, according to Ike. They managed to put some miles between themselves and Speight's canyon, though, so Adelita suggested that they make camp and get an early start the next day.

They found a place that was rocky enough to give them some protection, with yucca plants and brush all around. Adelita said it seemed safe enough to her, and Fargo agreed.

Against Ike's wishes they propped him up with his back to a rock and tied his feet.

"I'm not going to run off," he said. "I told you I'd take you to the guns, and I will."

"I hope you don't," Alvie said, making sure the knots in the ropes on Ike's feet were secure. "I'd sure like to see what the señorita can do to you with that whip."

"You old goat. You probably can't find yours without a search party."

"Wouldn't want you in the party," Alvie said. "You might want to watch your mouth if you want anybody to feed you. Sure hard to eat with both hands tied together."

"You wouldn't starve me," Ike said.

"You wait and see," Alvie told him.

They didn't let Ike go without food, however. When the beans were heated, Fargo untied his hands and watched him eat. After Ike finished, Fargo took the tin plate and tied Ike's hands again.

"We better find those guns before noon tomorrow," Fargo told him. "Adelita's getting impatient."

"I'll take you to 'em," Ike said. "You'll see."

"I hope so," Fargo said.

Adelita set her men to watch after they'd eaten, and before midnight Fargo came awake as she approached his bedroll, which he'd set well away from the others, just in case.

"You are awake," Adelita said as she lay down beside him.

"I sure am," Fargo said.

Adelita settled herself comfortably. "Do you believe that Ike will take us to the guns?"

Fargo laced his fingers together and put his hands behind his head. He looked up at the sky full of stars and the sinking moon.

"I believe he wants us to think he'll take us. I don't know what else he might have in mind, but you can bet it's something. He's not one to give up."

"There is no one to save him here. My men and I will not. You and Alvie will not."

"I know, but so far Ike's been mighty lucky. He could be counting on being lucky one more time."

"It will not happen. But you, that is a different story."

"You think I might get lucky?"

"I know you will."

Fargo had had that thought, too, and when Adelita's fingers sought him he was ready. His shaft was erect and waiting for her touch.

"Ummmm," she said, and she bent over Fargo to kiss him. His hand came from behind his head to go under her loose shirt and caress her engorged breasts, then tease the burning nipples.

Adelita held the kiss for a while before breaking away and stripping off her shirt. She shucked her pants, and said, "Stand up, Fargo."

It was an order Fargo didn't mind obeying. He stood up and pulled her to him, and they pressed against one another. Fargo's hot shaft lay in a line against Adelita's stomach, and he felt the wiry bush tingle his scrotum.

"How much of a man are you, Fargo?" Adelita said. "Enough to take me right now, as we are?"

"More than enough," he said.

He backed away a few inches, allowing his stiff rod to spring out. Adelita leaned down and took it in her mouth. She worked expertly for a few seconds before looking up at Fargo.

"You are ready?"

Fargo was ready. Even sex seemed to be a matter of testing with Adelita, but he didn't mind. He knew he would pass.

Adelita stood up and put her hands on his shoulders. Fargo took hold of her hips and lifted. The tip of his shaft was tickled by the hair at the entrance to her honey vault, but it didn't linger there. Fargo lowered her onto it, feeling the slickery sides, and she sighed.

"You are very strong, but will you be able to stand when we are done?"

"We'll find out," Fargo said.

He lifted her hips. Her hands were still on his shoulders, so she helped by raising herself. Soon they had attained a smooth rhythm, with Adelita throwing in an occasional twist or turn as the pleasure spasms took her. Her nipples burned a pair of paths up and down his chest. Her feet never touched the ground.

"This . . . is . . . so . . . good," she whispered.

Fargo thought so, too, but he saved his breath for the exertions. He didn't want things to end too soon.

Adelita didn't appear to want them to end, either, at least not at first. After a short while, however, her hips ground hard against him at each downward motion, and her breath came faster. She began to gasp, and Fargo rose on his toes to thrust into her.

"*Ay, Dios mío!*" she cried, and her entire body started to quiver. Fargo held her to him, and released the pent-up fire within him, jolt after jolt.

Finally, he was drained, and Adelita collapsed against him.

"You still stand," she whispered.

"Not for long," Fargo said.

He lowered her to the blanket and joined her there.

"Truly I have never met a man like you," Adelita said. "If Mexico were filled with such men, Benito Juárez would win most easily."

"With a woman like you on his side," Fargo said, "he will win without my help."

Adelita smiled and kissed him. "You are gallant, as well. Do you have Spanish blood?"

"Not that I know of, but I don't know a lot about my family."

Fargo's family had been lost to him so many years ago that even the memory of them had dimmed. It was a long story, and Fargo didn't feel like telling it. Fortunately Adelita didn't ask him to.

"They must have been of good stock to produce a man like you," she said.

"I like to think so," Fargo said as she wrapped her fingers around his shaft and he began to harden again.

10

Adelita had been gone for an hour when Fargo sat up and looked around. A noise had broken through his sleep, a noise that was out of the ordinary, and he wasted no time in slipping on his pants, pulling on his boots, and taking his Colt in his hand.

He moved soundlessly through the night and awoke Alvie and Adelita. Both saw the big revolver, and neither asked any questions.

Next, Fargo checked on the prisoner.

Ike was gone.

Fargo bit back a curse. His exertions with Adelita had caused him to sleep more soundly than usual or likely he would have heard something sooner.

He told Adelita and Alvie what had happened, and Adelita roused her men as quietly as she could while Alvie and Fargo went to check on the guards. They found them both, each one sitting with his back against a rock, each one with his throat cut.

"Speight," Alvie said. "He might not have many men left, but the ones he has are killers. They're like the Comanches, move like ghosts."

That wasn't any comfort to Fargo. Speight probably didn't even want the guns, but he wasn't going to let Fargo have them. He'd use Ike to get them, and after that he'd kill Ike.

"What're we gonna do?" Alvie asked. "Reckon we can track 'em in the dark?"

Fargo looked at the sky. "It won't be dark long."

"How many men you reckon Speight has left?"

"Enough to do to us what we did to him."

"Ambush us, you mean?"

"I expect him to try."

"We'd better be careful, then, 'cause I know we're goin' after him." Alvie paused. "We are goin' after him, ain't we?"

"Damn right," Fargo said.

Ike was scared, but his mind was working. He was sure he could come up with a plan. He had to.

Things had happened fast at the camp. He'd been half asleep and dreaming when someone clasped a big hand over his mouth and dragged him away. At first he'd thought his cousins had come for him and were taking him away from Fargo and that Mexican woman with the whip, but that was all just part of a dream.

Now that he was fully awake, he realized the awful truth. He was back in the hands of Speight and his Comancheros.

After a while, the man who'd grabbed him had tossed him over his shoulder like a sack of corn and carried him for half a mile as easily as if Ike had been a feather. Then he'd tossed him into a wagon, climbed into the seat, and driven away.

They'd gone another half mile or so before they met up with Speight and some other riders.

"Any trouble?" Speight asked.

His voice was flat, toneless, and dead, just as it had been when Ike was in the canyon.

"Nope," the big man said, shifting in the wagon seat. "Nobody turned a hair. How 'bout you all?"

Speight didn't answer him, nor did anyone else. Speight climbed down off his horse and got into the wagon with Ike, whose hands and feet were still bound.

Speight sat beside Ike. He wore a bloody shirt, and in his hand he held a bowie knife. Its wide blade glinted in the light of the fading moon. Speight touched the point of the knife to Ike's cheek.

"You have a choice to make," Speight said. "Do you want to hear what it is?"

Ike was afraid to nod, what with the knife being where it was, and his mouth was so dry that he wasn't sure he could talk. He worked up a little spit and said, "Tell me," his voice not much more than a croak.

"It's simple," Speight said. He caressed Ike's cheek with the flat of the blade. "You tell me where the guns are. Right now." He put the edge of the blade to Ike's throat. "Or I kill you. Right now."

Ike swallowed. The blade of the knife didn't move away from his throat.

"Don't tell me you don't know where they are," Speight said. "If you do, I'll kill you. Right here. Right now. I should have done it to begin with. Ah, well. 'Any man can make mistakes, but only an idiot persists in his error.' That's from Cicero. You wouldn't know about him."

Ike didn't give a hoot in hell about Cicero. He just wanted to stay alive, but he still had no plan. His mind churned, but nothing came to him. He was either going to die, or he was going to tell Speight about the guns. What the hell? He'd been about to tell him in the canyon before Fargo had come along.

"I'll tell you where the guns are," he said.

"I thought you might," Speight said.

He didn't put the knife away. He sat waiting for Ike to answer.

Ike described the place where he'd hidden the wagon. He told Speight the direction he'd traveled to get to the canyon. That was all he had to say.

"That's not good enough," Speight said.

"It's the best I can do."

"That may well be. Or it may be that you're simply trying to stay alive."

"It's all I can tell you," Ike said. "I swear."

"All right," Speight said. "I'll believe you, but if we don't find the guns by noon, you'll die."

Ike felt desperation take hold of him. "I thought you didn't even care about the guns."

"I don't." Speight put away the bowie knife and touched his shoulder. "But I don't like being shot, even if it's just a scratch, and I don't like having my men killed. I don't like having my camp burned and my horses stampeded. I don't like that at all. The man who did those things wants the guns. I'm going to take them from him, and then I'm going to kill him."

"Let me help you," Ike said.

"Help me?"

"Kill Fargo. That's the man who wants the guns. His name's Fargo. I want to kill him, too, but it ain't easy."

"It will be easy enough for me. He'll be following us. He'll die."

The way Speight said it, it sounded like an established fact. Ike thought he and Speight could get along just fine if only they hadn't gotten off on the wrong foot with each other.

"Listen," Ike said, a plan starting to take form, "you and I want the same thing, when you think about it. To kill Fargo. I don't care about the guns anymore. You can have the damn things. Just let me help you kill Fargo, and I'll go away. We'll both get what we want, and I'll just go away."

"I'll give it some thought," Speight said.

Fargo picked up the trail of the men who'd killed the guards easily enough. He found where it joined another trail, the one left by Speight and his gang, and he found the spot where they'd been joined by a wagon.

"I knew you were good," Alvie said, "but I didn't know you was this good."

"I think he is not so good," Adelita said. "I think even I could have followed this trail."

It bothered Fargo a little that she was right. The trail was so plain that anyone could have followed it. Speight had taken no trouble at all to conceal it or make it hard to find even at night. Fargo didn't like that.

"Well, Fargo," Adelita asked, "do you think I am as great a tracker as you?"

"I think it's a trap," Fargo said.

"Trap?" Alvie said, looking around. There wasn't a lot to see. It was full daylight now, and all around them were rocks and cactus and dry, dusty soil. "What kind of trap?"

"Speight wants us to follow him," Fargo said. "He thinks we'll come right on along, and he'll be waiting for us."

"Where?"

"Somewhere. What do you think, Adelita?"

"I think you are right."

She called to her men, who rode over and sat on their horses to await what she had to tell them. She repeated what Fargo had said, and they nodded in agreement.

"They think you are right, too," she told Fargo. "Now what shall we do about it?"

"You're going to ride into the trap," Fargo said.

"What's that supposed to mean?" Alvie asked.

"Just what I said. You're going to ride in. I won't be with you."

Alvie shook his head. "There's somethin' about that plan I don't much like."

"You'll like it better when I tell you more about it."

"I sure as hell hope so," Alvie said.

Alvie rode at the front of the little group as they approached the hill where the wagon was hidden. The trail they'd been following plainly led them there. Alvie was sweating, and not just because the sun was hot.

"What if they counted us last night?" he'd asked Fargo. "They'll know we're a couple of people short."

"You really think Ike's that smart?" Fargo asked.

"Prob'ly he ain't."

"And Speight didn't have a chance to count us, so he won't know. Besides, they won't be counting us now. They won't realize we know they're going to ambush us."

"Maybe so, but if they do figger it out, I'm the fella in front. I'm the one's gonna get shot and killed."

"Could be they'll just wing you," Fargo said.

"You sure do know how to cheer a fella up."

"Don't worry about it. You'll be fine."

Easy enough for Fargo to say, Alvie thought. Fargo wasn't the one who'd be leading a little bunch of Mexicans into a trap.

Alvie put up his hand and brought his horse to a stop. Adelita's men stopped right behind him, and Alvie peered ahead. He could see a hill and a lot of rocks. Two men were doing something at the base of the hill, and Alvie thought he could see a cave or something where the wagon might be hidden. He didn't see anything else. He guessed he was supposed to believe that the two men pretending to be busy were the only ones there, but he knew better. The others were hiding somewhere close by, either among the rocks or behind the hill.

Alvie didn't like anything about the situation, but he wasn't the one running the show. That was Fargo's job, and the Trailsman had said not to worry. He'd said everything would be fine.

Alvie hoped he was right about that.

Fargo's plan was simple. Since Speight was leading them in a straight line, Fargo wasn't going to follow the trail. He and Adelita would loop around and come up behind Speight.

There were any number of things wrong with the plan. It would take some hard riding, and Fargo would have to guess at where Speight would be holed up. He'd also have to count on the fact that Speight would never think someone could sneak up on him from behind twice in a couple of days.

When they had come to within a mile of the hill, Fargo had seen it in the distance. The rocks all around made it a perfect spot for an ambush, so Fargo was pretty sure that would be the place where Speight was set up. It might even be the place where the guns were hidden.

Fargo and Adelita broke away from the group and started on their loop.

"What if you're wrong?" Adelita asked as they rode.

"Then I'm wrong. If you have a better idea, now's the time to tell me."

"I have no better idea. I just wondered what we would do."

"We'll try something else," Fargo said, "but I don't think I'm wrong."

"Tell me the rest of the plan, then."

"You see that hill?"

They were well away from it, far enough that Fargo hoped that Speight and his men, if they were there, wouldn't notice them.

"I see it," Adelita said.

"We're going to circle around behind it, come over the top, and surprise Speight. He'll be in front of it with his men, hiding in the rocks."

Adelita got the idea. "We will kill as many as we can, and my men will ride in and take care of the rest."

"That's about the size of it," Fargo said.

Adelita looked doubtful. "I suppose it is worth a try."

"Better than nothing."

"But not much," Adelita said.

Ike had a plan, too. He'd thought about it all the way to the place where the guns were hidden, and Speight had done exactly what Ike thought he would. He'd told Ike he'd have to clear the brush and hitch up the mules, which Speight had brought along. That would put Ike right out in front when the shooting started, and Ike knew the shooting would indeed start. Speight was leaving a trail a blind man could follow, and he was hoping Fargo would come along and fall into a trap. He was probably also hoping that Ike would be the first man shot. Ike didn't intend to let that happen.

"I can't do all that by myself," Ike said. "I need some help."

"You help him, Grunt," Speight said.

Grunt was the big man driving the wagon. He had a recently broken nose that was still bruised and misshapen. Ike thought he was the man Fargo had kicked in the face as they made their escape from Speight's camp.

"I don't like it," Grunt said.

"But you'll do it," Speight said, and his voice was deader than Ike had ever heard it.

"Sure, sure. I'll do it. I just don't like it."

"You don't have to like it," Speight said, and that was the end of it.

When they'd arrived at the hill, Speight had scattered his men around behind the rocks nearby. One of them had taken the horses around the hill with orders to stay with them. Speight cut the ropes that held Ike, and while Ike tried to rub some circulation into his hands and feet, Speight told him what to expect. It was pretty much what Ike had thought he'd say.

"There's going to be shooting, but you're not to do any fighting. If you survive and if Fargo is dead, you can leave. I'll take the rifles with me."

"You'll leave me a horse," Ike said.

"Of course."

Ike nodded, though he knew Speight was lying. He'd kill Ike and leave him where he lay if Ike wasn't killed sooner.

We'll see about that, Ike thought.

Fargo and Adelita spotted the man with the horses easily. Getting rid of him without alerting Speight and the others was the problem.

"I will take care of it," Adelita said.

"You sure?" Fargo said. "He's likely to shoot you as soon as he sees you."

Adelita laughed. "I do not think so. He is a man. Easy to fool. You stay out of sight."

Fargo rode the big Ovaro behind a boulder, and Adelita rode toward the horses. As she got closer, she began to unbutton her shirt.

The man raised his rifle, but then he lowered it. He hadn't been expecting a woman, and he certainly hadn't expected one who was exposing her bountiful breasts for his admiration.

Adelita removed her hat and shook out her hair. She shrugged the shirt off her shoulders. The man was frozen in place. It was as if his feet were nailed to the ground.

Adelita rode closer. The man was eager to see more of her, but he didn't put down the rifle. When Adelita was nearly upon him, she smiled and beckoned to him. He somehow managed to step forward.

The whip appeared in Adelita's hand as if by magic, snaking out and wrapping itself around the man's neck. Adelita pulled the horse's head to the right, and the horse jumped in that direction.

Fargo thought he heard the man's spine snap, but it might have been just his imagination. He rode out from behind the boulder and joined Adelita, who was calmly buttoning her shirt.

"You see?" she said. "Easy." She slid off her horse and retrieved the whip. "Now we will take care of the others."

"Sure enough," Fargo said.

He joined her on the ground, and they climbed the hill. It was easy going, and when they arrived at the crest, they were able to conceal themselves in the brush and look down at what was going on below.

Fargo saw that Alvie and his small band of men were sitting their horses in the distance, not moving. Speight and his men waited patiently, hidden in the rocks.

Fargo couldn't see Ike, but he could see a couple of mules directly below the hill. They appeared to be hitched to something, and Fargo decided that the wagon must be hidden there.

It went against his grain to kill men without giving them some sort of warning, and he would have called out had Adelita not begun shooting. She didn't have the same scruples that Fargo did, and she'd shot a man before Fargo had time to say a word.

Even as the man was falling, Speight and his men turned

and started firing up the hill. Alvie and his group charged forward, guns blasting.

In the midst of all the shooting, the wagon loaded with the rifles came rumbling from the side of the hill. Ike sat in the wagon seat, whipping the mules with the reins, urging them to run as fast as they could. The gunfire all around them gave them an added reason to put on speed, and the wagon moved away in a cloud of dust.

It appeared that Ike was caught in a cross fire, but as soon as he cleared the rocks, he turned the wagon sharply to the left and headed for the open country.

"You must stop him, Fargo," Adelita said.

Fargo ran back down the hill and jumped on the Ovaro. When he rounded the hill, he saw the wagon bouncing along swiftly, accompanied by its dust cloud.

Fargo urged his big horse on. If the Ovaro stepped in a hole, it would be the end of both him and Fargo, but the Trailsman had no intention of letting Ike get away, no matter the risk.

The wagon bounced and swayed, and as Fargo got closer, he could see that Ike was having a tough time keeping it from turning over and losing its load.

Ike lashed the mules with the reins, but they were going as fast as they could with their heavy load, and Fargo caught them quickly. He rode along beside Ike and shouted, "Stop right here, Ike!"

Ike didn't even look at him, and he didn't slow down.

Fargo wished he had Adelita's whip, but since he didn't, he pulled his Colt. He didn't want to kill Ike. He wanted to take him back to San Antonio for his trial.

Ike wasn't armed, but Fargo couldn't get hold of the reins to stop the mules. He thought about trying to jump onto the load of guns and stop Ike that way, but that was too chancy. He figured he'd have to shoot Ike and hope he didn't kill him. It was hard to be accurate when you were shooting at a moving target from a running horse.

But Ike saved Fargo from having to shoot. He was so eager to get away that he'd forgotten all about caution. The left front wagon wheel hit a hole, and the whole back end of the wagon lifted into the air.

Ike flew off the seat and landed ten feet away. The wagon bounced and kept on going.

Fargo went after it. He caught up within a quarter of a mile and was able to get hold of the reins that lay across the back of one of the mules. He took hold of them and pulled. It wasn't as easy as it would have been if he'd been in the seat, but he brought the mules to a stop. They stood and breathed heavily, their sides heaving. Fargo didn't think they'd have lasted much longer. Ike had driven them so hard that their lungs had about burst.

Fargo left them and rode back to see about Ike. The would-be gunrunner lay with his face twisted toward Fargo. His head was beside a rock. There was blood on the rock and on the ground.

"Didn't work out like I planned," Ike said. His voice was barely a whisper. "Don't guess you'll be taking me back to San Antonio with you, though."

The Trailsman looked down at him. "Maybe we can fix you up."

"Doubt it. Almost had those damn guns. If it wasn't for you, I'd . . ."

Ike didn't finish the sentence, and he wouldn't be talking anymore to anybody. Fargo left the mules and the wagon and rode back to see about Alvie and Adelita.

* * *

Speight and his men, the few that remained, stood in front of the opening in the hillside. One of the men was Grunt, his nose freshly broken. They were all roped together so that they could move around a bit, but not much.

"Where are the guns?" Adelita asked as soon as Fargo was within hearing distance.

"They're all right. The mules needed a rest."

"We can use this one's horses to pull the wagon," Adelita said, pointing at Speight.

"Take two of the horses and go for the wagon," she told one of her men. He motioned to another man, and they went to get the horses.

"What about Ike?" Alvie asked.

"Dead," Fargo said.

"I guess that pays for Harl," Alvie said. "Seems fair enough to me."

"Best we can do," Fargo said.

"Skye Fargo," Speight said, his voice flat and cold. "You'd best kill me now, or I'll have my revenge."

"Maybe so, maybe not," Fargo said. "You have a long way to walk without water and food. Might not make it. Hard to walk, all tied up like that."

"You'd best untie us."

"Nope. I'll leave that to you to work out among yourselves." Fargo turned to Alvie. "You ready to go back to San Antonio?"

"Sure am," Alvie said.

"You have been a great help, Fargo," Adelita said. "If you are ever in Mexico, Benito Juárez could use a man like you." She smiled. "So, too, could I."

"I'll be sure to look for you if I ever get down below the border," Fargo said.

"I hope you will." Adelita turned to address her remaining men. "Let us go to the rifles. *Vamanos*."

Alvie and Fargo watched her ride away.

"Sure 'nuff a lot of woman there," Alvie said. "I'd be tempted to go along with her if I was you."

Fargo thought about San Antonio, about Michelle Charboneau, and about Frances Martin.

"I think I'll go on back with you," he said. "I have a couple of things to take care of in San Antonio."

"I'll just bet you do," Alvie said. "Let's get on the way."

They rode east, and neither one looked back at Speight and his men.

Or at Adelita.

LOOKING FORWARD!
**The following is the opening
section of the next novel in the exciting
Trailsman series from Signet:**

**TRAILSMAN #356
GRIZZLY FURY**

*1861, the northern Rockies—where fang and claw
make a feast of human flesh.*

The first to die was a prospector. Old Harry, folks called him.
Elk hunters were near his diggings and decided to pay him a
visit. Everyone liked the old man. He could spin yarns by the
hour.

His yarn-spinning days were over. They found Old Harry's
legs near his cabin. A blood trail led to an arm and more blood
led to the rest of him. His head had been split open and his
brains apparently eaten.

The tracks of the culprit were plain enough. Old Harry's
attacker was a bear. Judging by the size of the prints it was a
grizzly. An exceptionally large grizzly, but then, large bears
were nothing new in the mountains that far north.

The hunters buried the remains and went on with their hunt.

The bear was long gone and they figured they had nothing to worry about. They found elk and shot a bull and skinned it and dried and salted the meat. There were five of them with families to feed so one elk wasn't enough. Four hunters went off the next day while the fifth man stayed at camp. The four returned toward sunset, worn and tired and hungry and empty-handed, to find their camp in a shambles and their companion missing. Their effects had been torn apart. The racks of elk meat had been shattered. They looked for their friend and finally came on parts of his body in a ravine. It was Old Harry all over again, only worse. His head, too, had been split like a melon, and the brains devoured.

The hunters got out of there. They rode like madmen the twenty-five miles down to Gold Creek and told everyone what had happened. It was the talk of the town for weeks and then they had new things to talk about.

Bear attacks were common enough that the deaths didn't alarm them.

Then one evening a horse came limping into town. It was lathered with sweat and bleeding from claw marks. Some of them knew the man who owned it. A large party hurried to his cabin four miles up the creek.

The front door had been busted in. Inside was horror. Blood was everywhere, along with bits and pieces of the victim.

That a bear was to blame was obvious. That it was the same bear occurred to them when they found that the man's brains had been scooped out.

They realized the grizzly must have followed the elk hunters down. That was unusual but not remarkable. They thought they were dealing with an ordinary bear and organized a hunt to put an end to the man killer before anyone else died.

Fifty men bristling with weapons rode out to wage battle with the beast. They used dogs to follow the trail, big, fearless dogs that had gone after other bears and mountain lions many a time. The dogs found the scent and their owner let them loose and for over a mile their baying showed they were hard after their quarry.

The men hurried to catch up. They were excited and confident and told one another that the grizzly was fit to be stuffed and mounted.

When the howls changed to yowls of terror, it stopped them in their tracks. They sat breathless and still as the screams and shrieks seemed to go on forever. When silence fell they cautiously advanced.

It was as bad as they imagined it would be. The dogs had been slaughtered. For half an acre the ground was a jigsaw of legs and tails and ribs and bodies. They tried to take up the trail without the dogs but they soon lost it.

For a few days Gold Creek was as quiet as a church. But these were hardy men and women, used to life in the wild, and gradually their lives returned to normal.

A couple of weeks passed. One day smoke was seen rising above a cabin along the creek. So much smoke, it drew others to investigate. The cabin was in flames. They yelled for the prospector who lived there but he didn't answer. They reckoned he must have knocked a lamp over and they worried that he was still inside and had been burned to death. Then someone noticed blood and they followed it into the trees. The remains were like a trail of bread crumbs. Here an arm, there a leg, at another spot a foot. The torso was whole, which surprised them. The brains were missing, which didn't.

A town meeting was called. Everyone agreed this was a

serious situation. Four people and seven good dogs were dead.

They decided to send for the best bear hunter in the territory.

His fee was a hundred dollars but that was money well spent if they could be rid of the grizzly.

The bear hunter came. He brought his own dogs, four of the largest and meanest-looking hounds anyone had ever saw. He spent an evening drinking and boasting of his prowess and the next morning he and his mean-looking hounds rode off after the bear.

No one ever set eyes on the hunter or his dogs again.

About a month after the bear hunter disappeared, two men going up the creek to their claim happened on a dead mule. Its throat had been ripped out. Its owner, or rather, parts of him, lay nearby. He had a hole in the top of his head as big around as a pie pan. And no brain.

Another hunt was organized. Every last man who lived in or around Gold Creek was required to report with a rifle and be mustered into what the town council called the Bear Militia. They took to the field with high hopes. Every square foot for miles was scoured. They didn't find so much as a fresh track.

The hunt was deemed a success. They told themselves that their show of force had scared the bear off, that they were shed of it once and for all.

The next morning the parson rode out to visit an elderly woman and her husband. The woman was sickly and the parson paid daily visits to bolster her spirits. Their cabin was less than a quarter of a mile from Gold Creek. He knew something was wrong when he saw that the door hung by a hinge.

Clutching his Bible, the parson made bold to poke his head in. He promptly drew it out again, and retched.

Yet another town meeting was called. Enough was enough, everyone agreed. The way things were going, pretty soon the grizzly would be breaking into homes in town. Something had to be done.

Gold Creek was prosperous. They had six hundred dollars in the treasury but they didn't think that was enough. They took up a collection that brought the total to a thousand. The mayor thought that was piddling. They needed the best and the best didn't come cheap. He reminded them of how many had lost their lives, and how many more might lose theirs, and called on everyone to do their civic duty and donate as much as they could afford. He also threatened to close the saloons until he had a large enough sum to suit him.

A week later the flyers went out. They were sent to news-papers far and wide, announcing that a five-thousand-dollar bounty had been placed on the grizzly that was terrorizing Gold Creek.

They even gave the bear a name.

They called it Brain Eater.

Skye Fargo came up the trail from Fort Flathead. He swung around Flathead Lake and followed Swann River to the mountains. Instead of crossing over Maria Pass to the other side of the divide, he took the trail that led north and in a few days reached Gold Creek.

From a distance it looked like any other boom town except that most of the buildings were made from logs. At the south end stood an exception, a church with a steeple. There were a few houses, too, that boasted of the prosperity of their owners.

Flowing past the town from the north was the ribbon of water that accounted for much of Gold Creek's wealth.

Fargo gigged the Ovaro down the mountain. A big man, he wore buckskins and a red bandanna. A Colt was strapped around his waist and the stock of a rifle jutted from his saddle scabbard. His lake blue eyes missed little as he passed outlying cabins and shacks and entered the town.

He was pleased to see so many saloons; six, by his count. It suggested to him that like many frontier settlements, the people of Gold Creek revered the Lord on Sunday and raised holy hell the rest of the week.

A portly man in a bowler was crossing the street and nodded as he went by.

"Ask you a question, mister," Fargo said, drawing rein.

The man had florid cheeks and ferret eyes. He stopped and looked Fargo up and down and said, "Another one, by God."

"Another what?" Fargo said, not sure he liked the man's tone.

"Another fool after that damn griz," the man said. "Or am I mistaken?"

"It's not dead yet?" Fargo wanted to know. He'd hate to think he had come all this way for nothing.

The man snorted. "Mister, that bear is Satan incarnate. You ask me, the bullet hasn't been made that will bring him low."

Fargo bent and patted the stock of his rifle. "I aim to give it a try."

"You and fifty others. Our town is crawling with bear hunters, thanks to that flyer we never should have sent out. My name is Petty, by the way. Theodore Petty. I own the general store. I also happen to be the mayor."

"You don't want the hunters here?"

"At first I did. I put five hundred dollars toward the bounty, thinking it was for the best. Had I known the kind of people it would bring I wouldn't have done it. But enough idle chat. My advice to you is to turn around and leave. Five of the hunters have already died and you could be the sixth."

"The griz has killed five more?"

"Actually, the total is eleven. But no. Only two of them were hunters. Another was killed in a drunken fight in a saloon and two more had a falling-out over how they were going to split the five thousand dollars and shot themselves dead." Petty touched his bowler's brim. "Good day to you, sir."

Fargo digested the news as he rode to a hitch rail in front of one of the saloons and dismounted. Tying off the reins, he stretched. The saloon was called *The Sluice*. He pushed on the batwings. Although it was barely noon the place was crowded. He bellied up to the bar and paid for a bottle. Since he couldn't find an empty chair, he went back out and sat on an upended crate and savored his first swallow of red-eye in more than a week.

"Well, now, what have we here?"

Fargo cocked an eye over the bottle at a young woman in a gay yellow dress, holding a yellow parasol. Brunette curls fanned from under a matching yellow bonnet. She was appraising him as a horse buyer might a stud stallion. "Didn't your ma ever warn you about talking to strange men?"

"She did, indeed," the woman said. "But I always make exceptions for handsome men, and God Almighty, you are one handsome son of a bitch."

Fargo laughed and introduced himself.

"I'm Fanny Jellico," she said with a twirl of her parasol.

"Let me guess. You're here after Brain Eater?"

Nodding, Fargo said, "You too, I take it?"

Now it was Fanny who laughed. She leaned her back to the wall, closed her parasol, and surveyed the busy street. "It's become a circus. I suppose I shouldn't complain since we've got more business than we can handle but it's almost as dangerous in town as it is out there in the woods with the bear."

"We?" Fargo said.

"Me and a bunch of girls came all the way from Denver," Fanny explained. "It was Madame Basque's doing. She runs a sporting house. When she saw that flyer she knew there was money to be made. So she loaded eight of us into a wagon and here we are."

"That's a long way to come."

"Maybe so," Fanny said. "But we're making money hand over thigh."

Fargo chuckled. "The marshal and the parson don't mind?"

"There isn't any law," Fanny revealed. "The town never got around to appointing one. As for the parson"—she gazed down the street at the church then looked at Fargo and winked—"he's as friendly as can be."

"I hear there's been a knifing and a shooting."

"Hell, there have been twenty or more just since we came," Fanny said. "The hunters spend more time fighting amongst themselves than they do hunting the bear. And I use the word 'hunter' loosely. Some of them couldn't find their own ass if they were told where it is."

Fargo was beginning to understand why Theodore Petty

resented the influx of bounty seekers. Gold Creek had gone from a run-of-the-mill mountain town to a wild and wooly pit of violence and carnal desire. Just the kind of place he liked most.

"If you're interested in a good time, you might look me up at the Three Deuces. Madam Basque made an arrangement where we use the rooms in the back. I'm there from six until midnight most every night."

"I might just do that."

Fanny brazenly traced the outline of his jaw with a finger.

"I might just let you have me at a discount, as good-looking as you are."

The next instant the front window exploded with a tremendous crash. Fargo sprang to his feet and simultaneously Fanny screamed and threw herself against him. Both watched a man tumble to a stop in the street and lay half-dazed.

Through the shattered window strode a colossus. Seven feet tall if he was an inch, he wore a buffalo robe and a floppy hat. Tucked under his belt was an armory: two pistols, two knives, and a hatchet. He walked over to the man in the street and declared, "Get up and get your due."

The man rolled over. Buckskins clad his wiry frame. He was getting on in years and had hair as white as snow. He had a lot of wrinkles, too. Propping himself on his elbows, he wiped a sleeve across his mouth, smearing the blood that dribbled over his lower lip. "You shouldn't ought to have done that, Moose."

"You say mean things, you should expect it," the man mountain declared.

Fargo pried Fanny's fingers from his arm. "Hold this," he

said, and gave her the bottle. Moving out from under the overhang, he walked over to the old man. "Rooster Strimm," he said. "It's been a coon's age."

Rooster blinked and grinned. "Why, look who it is. Ain't seen you since Green River."

Moose didn't like the interruption. "You know this feller?" he said to Rooster.

"I surely do," the old man confirmed. "He's a friend of mine. Skye Fargo, meet Moose Taylor."

Moose turned. "Friend or not, you'd better back away. Rooster, here, was mean to me and I don't like it when folks are mean. I aim to hurt him some and there's nothing you can do to stop me."

"Care to bet?" Fargo said.